MISS PRIM'S GREEK ISLAND FLING

MISS PRIM'S GREEK ISLAND FLING

MICHELLE DOUGLAS

MILLS & BOON

First published in Great Britain 2019
by Mills & Boon, an imprint of HarperCollins*Publishers*
1 London Bridge Street, London, SE1 9GF

Large Print edition 2019

© 2019 Michelle Douglas

ISBN: 978-0-263-08280-7

MIX
Paper from
responsible sources
FSC® C007454

Printed and bound in Great Britain
by CPI Group (UK) Ltd, Croydon, CR0 4YY

To Pam, who is always happy to share
a bottle of red and to talk
into the wee small hours of the night.

CHAPTER ONE

IT WAS THE sound of shattering glass that woke her.

Audra shot bolt upright in bed, heart pounding, praying that the sound had been a part of one of her frequent nightmares, but knowing deep down in her bones—in all the places where she knew such things were real—that it wasn't.

A thump followed. Something heavy being dropped to the floor. And then a low, jeering voice. The sound of cupboard doors opening and closing.

She'd locked all the doors and windows downstairs! She'd been hyper-vigilant about such things ever since she'd arrived two days ago. She glanced at her bedroom window, at the curtain moving slowly on a draught of warm night air, and called herself a fool for leaving it open. Anyone could have climbed up onto the first-floor balcony and gained entry.

Slipping out of bed, she grabbed her phone and held it pressed hard against her chest as she crept out into the hallway. As the only person in residence in Rupert's Greek villa, she'd seen no reason to close her bedroom door, which at least meant she didn't have to contend with the sound of it creaking open now.

She'd chosen the bedroom at the top of the stairs and from this vantage point she could see a shadow bounce in and out of view from the downstairs living room. She heard Rupert's liquor cabinet being opened and the sound of a glass bottle being set down. Thieves were stealing her brother's much-loved single malt whisky?

Someone downstairs muttered something in… French?

She didn't catch what was said.

Someone answered back in Greek.

She strained her ears, but could catch no other words. So…there were two of them? She refused to contemplate what would happen if they found her here—a lone woman. Swallowing down a hard knot of fear, she made her way silently down the hallway, away from the stairs, to the farthest room along—the master bedroom. The door made the softest of snicks as she eased it closed. In the moonlight she made out the walk-in wardrobe on the other side of the room and headed straight for it, closing that door behind her, fighting to breathe through the panic that weighed her chest down.

She dialled the emergency number. 'Please help me,' she whispered in Greek. 'Please. There are intruders in my house.' She gave her name. She gave the address. The operator promised that someone was on the way and would be there in minutes. She spoke in reassuringly calm tones. She asked Audra where in the house she was, and if there was anywhere she could hide. She told Audra to stay on the line and that helped too.

'I'm hiding in the walk-in wardrobe in the master bedroom.' And that was when it hit her. She was all but locked in a closet. *Again.* It made no difference that this time she'd locked herself in. Panic clawed at her throat as she recalled the suffocating darkness and the way her body had started to cramp after hours spent confined in her tiny hall closet. When Thomas had not only locked her in, but had left and she hadn't known if he would ever return to let her out again. And if he didn't return, how long would it take for anyone to find her? How long before someone raised the alarm? She'd spent hours in a terrified limbo—after screaming herself hoarse for help—where she'd had to fight for every breath. 'I can't stay here.'

'The police are almost there,' the operator assured her.

She closed her eyes. This wasn't her horridly cramped hall closet, but a spacious walk-in robe. It didn't smell of damp leather and fuggy cold. This smelled of…the sea. And she could stretch out her full length and not touch the other wall if she wanted to. Anger, cold and comforting, streaked through her then. Her eyes flew open. She would *not* be a victim again. Oh, she wasn't going to march downstairs and confront those two villains ransacking her brother's house, but she wasn't going to stay here, a cornered quaking mess either.

Her free hand clenched to a fist. *Think!* If she were a thief, what would she steal?

Electrical equipment—televisions, stereos and computers. Which were all downstairs. She grimaced. Except for the television on the wall in the master bedroom.

She'd bet they'd look for jewellery too. And where was the most likely place to find that? The master bedroom.

She needed to find a better hiding place—one that had an escape route if needed.

And she needed a weapon. Just in case. She didn't rate her chances against two burly men, but she could leave some bruises if they did try to attack her. She reminded herself that the police would be here soon.

For the first time since arriving in this island idyll, Audra cursed the isolation of Rupert's villa. It was the last property on a peninsula surrounded by azure seas. The glorious sea views, the scent of the ocean and gardens, the sound of lapping water combined with the humming of bees and the chattering of the birds had started to ease the burning in her soul. No media, no one hassling her for an interview, no flashing cameras whenever she strode outside her front door. The privacy had seemed like a godsend.

Until now.

Using the torch app on her phone, she scanned the wardrobe for something she could use to defend herself. Her fingers closed about a lacrosse stick. It must've been years since Rupert had played, and she had no idea what he was still doing with a stick now, but at the moment she didn't care.

Cracking open the wardrobe door, she listened for a full minute before edging across the room to the glass sliding door of the balcony. She winced at the click that seemed to echo throughout the room with a *come-and-find-me* din when she unlocked it, but thanked Rupert's maintenance man when it slid open on its tracks as silent as the moon. She paused and listened again for another full minute before easing outside and closing the door behind her. Hugging the shadows of the wall, she moved to the end of the balcony and inserted herself between two giant pot plants. The only way anyone would see her was if they came right out onto the balcony and moved in this direction. She gripped the lacrosse stick so tightly her fingers started to ache.

She closed her eyes and tried to get her breathing under control. The thieves would have no reason to come out onto the balcony. There was nothing to steal out here. And she doubted they'd be interested in admiring the view, regardless of how spectacular it might be. The tight band around her chest eased a fraction.

The flashing lights from the police car that tore into the driveway a moment later eased the tightness even further. She counted as four armed men piled out of the vehicle and headed straight inside. She heard shouts downstairs.

But still she didn't move.

After a moment she lifted the phone to her ear. 'Is it…is it safe to come out yet?' she whispered.

'One of the men has been apprehended. The

officers are searching for the second man.' There was a pause. 'The man they have in custody claims he's on his own.'

She'd definitely heard French *and* Greek.

'He also says he's known to your brother.'

'Known?' She choked back a snort. 'I can assure you that my brother doesn't associate with people who break into houses.'

'He says his name is Finn Sullivan.'

Audra closed her eyes. *Scrap that.* Her brother knew *one* person who broke into houses, and his name was Finn Sullivan.

Finn swore in French, and then in Greek for good measure, when he knocked the crystal tumbler from the bench to the kitchen tiles below, making a God-awful racket that reverberated through his head. It served him right for not switching on a light, but he knew Rupert's house as well as he knew his own, and he'd wanted to try to keep the headache stretching behind his eyes from building into a full-blown migraine.

Blowing out a breath, he dropped his rucksack to the floor and, muttering first in French and then in Greek, clicked on a light and retrieved the dustpan and brush to clean up the mess. For pity's sake. Not only hadn't Rupert's last house guest washed, dried and put away the tumbler—leaving it for him to break—but they hadn't taken out the garbage either! Whenever he stayed, Finn always made sure to leave the place exactly as he found it—spotlessly clean and tidy. He hated to think of his friend being taken advantage of.

Helping himself to a glass of Rupert's excellent whisky, Finn lowered himself into an armchair in the living room, more winded than he cared to admit. The cast had come off his arm yesterday and it ached like the blazes now. As did his entire left side and his left knee. Take it easy, the doctor had ordered. But he'd been taking it easy for eight long weeks. And Nice had started to feel like a prison.

Rupert had given him a key to this place a couple of years ago, and had told him to treat it as his own. He'd ring Rupert tomorrow to let him know he was here. He glanced at the clock on the wall. Two thirty-seven a.m. was too late…or early…to call anyone. He rested his head back and closed his eyes, and tried to will the pain coursing through his body away.

He woke with a start to flashing lights, and it took him a moment to realise they weren't due to a migraine. He blinked, but the armed policemen—two of them and each with a gun trained on him—didn't disappear. The clock said two forty-eight.

He raised his hands in the universal gesture of non-aggression. 'My name is Finn Sullivan,' he said in Greek. 'I am a friend of Rupert Russel, the owner of this villa.'

'Where is your accomplice?'

'Accomplice?' He stood then, stung by the fuss and suspicion. 'What accomplice?'

He wished he'd remained seated when he found himself tackled to the floor, pain bursting like red-hot needles all the way down his left side, magnifying the blue-black ache that made him want to roar.

He clamped the howls of pain behind his teeth and nodded towards his backpack as an officer rough-handled him to his feet after handcuffing him. 'My identification is in there.'

His words seemed to have no effect. One of the officers spoke into a phone. He was frogmarched into the grand foyer. Both policemen looked upwards expectantly, so he did too.

'Audra!'

Flanked by two more police officers, she pulled to a dead halt halfway down the stairs, her eyes widening—those too cool and very clear blue eyes. 'Finn?' Delicate nostrils flared. 'What on earth are you doing here?'

The glass on the sink, the litter in the kitchen bin made sudden sense. '*You* called the police?'

'Of course I called the police!'

'Of all the idiotic, overdramatic reactions! How daft can you get?' He all but yelled the words at her, his physical pain needing an outlet. 'Why the hell would you overreact like that?'

'Daft? Daft!' Her voice rose as she flew down the stairs. 'And what do you call breaking and entering my brother's villa at two thirty in the morning?'

It was probably closer to three by now. He didn't say that out loud. 'I didn't break in. I have a key.'

He saw then that she clutched a lacrosse stick. She looked as if she wouldn't mind cracking him over the head with it. With a force of effort he pulled in a breath. A woman alone in a deserted house…the sound of breaking glass… And after everything she'd been through recently…

He bit back a curse. He'd genuinely frightened her.

The pain in his head intensified. 'I'm sorry, Squirt.' The old nickname dropped from his lips. 'If I'd known you were here I'd have rung to let you know I was coming. In the meantime, can you tell these guys who I am and call them off?'

'Where's your friend?'

His shoulder ached like the blazes. He wanted to yell at her to get the police to release him. He bit the angry torrent back. Knowing Audra, she'd make him suffer as long as she could if he yelled at her again.

And he *was* genuinely sorry he'd frightened her.

'I came alone.'

'But I heard two voices—one French, one Greek.'

He shook his head. 'You heard one voice and two languages.' He demonstrated his earlier cussing fit, though he toned it down to make it more palatable for mixed company.

For a moment the knuckles on her right hand whitened where it gripped the lacrosse stick, and then relaxed. She told the police officers in perfect Greek how sorry she was to have raised a false alarm, promised to bake them homemade lemon drizzle cakes and begged them very nicely to let him go as he was an old friend of her brother's. He wasn't sure why, but it made him grind his teeth.

He groaned his relief when he was uncuffed,

rubbing his wrists rather than his shoulder, though he was damned if he knew why. Except he didn't want any of them to know how much he hurt. He was sick to death of his injuries.

A part of him would be damned too before it let Audra see him as anything but hearty and hale. Her pity would…

He pressed his lips together. He didn't know. All he knew was that he didn't want to become an object of it.

Standing side by side in the circular drive, they waved the police off. He followed her inside, wincing when she slammed the door shut behind them. The fire in her eyes hadn't subsided. 'You want to yell at me some more?'

He'd love to. It was what he and Audra did— they sniped at each other. They had ever since she'd been a gangly pre-teen. But he hurt too much to snipe properly. It was taking all his strength to control the nausea curdling his stomach. He glanced at her from beneath his shaggy fringe. Besides, it was no fun sniping at someone with the kind of shadows under their eyes that Audra had.

He eased back to survey her properly. She was too pale and too thin. He wasn't used to seeing her vulnerable and frightened.

Frighteningly efficient? *Yes.*

Unsmiling? *Yes.*

Openly disapproving of his lifestyle choices? *Double yes.*

But pale, vulnerable and afraid? *No.*

'That bastard really did a number on you, didn't he, Squirt?'

Her head reared back and he could've bitten his tongue out. 'Not quite as big a number as that mountain did on you, from all reports.'

She glanced pointedly at his shoulder and with a start he realised he'd been massaging it. He waved her words away. 'A temporary setback.'

She pushed out her chin. 'Ditto.'

The fire had receded from her eyes and this time it was he who had to suffer beneath their merciless ice-blue scrutiny. And that was when he realised that all she wore was a pair of thin cotton pyjama bottoms and a singlet top that moulded itself to her form. His tongue stuck to the roof of his mouth.

The problem with Audra was that she was *exactly* the kind of woman he went after. If he had a type it was the buttoned-up, repressed librarian type, and normally Audra embodied that to a tee. But at the moment she was about as far from that as you could get. She was all blonde sleep-tousled temptation and his skin prickled with an awareness that was both familiar and unfamiliar.

He had to remind himself that a guy didn't mess with his best friend's sister.

'Did the police hurt you?'

'Absolutely not.' He was admitting nothing.

She cocked an eyebrow. 'Finn, it's obvious you're in pain.'

He shrugged and then wished he hadn't when pain blazed through his shoulder. 'The cast only came off yesterday.'

Her gaze moved to his left arm. 'And instead of resting it, no doubt as your doctors suggested, you jumped on the first plane for Athens, caught the last ferry to Kyanós, grabbed a late dinner in the village and trekked the eight kilometres to the villa.'

'Bingo.' He'd relished the fresh air and the freedom. For the first two kilometres.

'While carrying a rucksack.'

Eight weeks ago he'd have been able to carry twice the weight for ten kilometres without breaking a sweat.

She picked up his glass of half-finished Scotch and strode into the kitchen. As she reached up into a kitchen cupboard her singlet hiked up to expose a band of perfect pale skin that had his gut clenching. She pulled out a packet of aspirin and sent it flying in a perfect arc towards him—he barely needed to move to catch it. And then she lifted his glass to her lips and drained it and stars burst behind his eyelids. It was the sexiest thing he'd ever seen.

She filled it with tap water and set it in front of him. 'Take two.'

He did as she ordered because it was easier than arguing with her. And because he hurt all over and it seemed too much trouble to find the heavy-duty painkillers his doctor had prescribed for him and which were currently rolling around in the bottom of his backpack somewhere.

'Which room do you usually use?'

'The one at the top of the stairs.'

'You're out of luck, buddy.' She stuck out a hip, and he gulped down more water. 'That's the one I'm using.'

He feigned outrage. 'But that one has the best view!' Which was a lie. All the upstairs bed-rooms had spectacular views.

She smirked. 'I know. First in and all that.'

He choked down a laugh. That was one of the things he'd always liked about Audra. She'd play along with him...all in the name of one-upmanship, of course.

'Right, which bedroom do you want? There are another three upstairs to choose from.' She strode around and lifted his bag. She grunted and had to use both hands. 'Yeah, right—light as a feather.'

He glanced at her arms. While the rucksack wasn't exactly light, it wasn't that heavy. She'd never been a weakling. She'd lost condition. He tried to recall the last time he'd seen her.

'Earth to Finn.'

He started. 'I'll take the one on the ground floor.' The one behind the kitchen. The only bedroom in the house that didn't have a sea view. The bedroom furthest away from Audra's. They wouldn't even have to share a bathroom if he stayed down here. Which would be for the best.

He glanced at that singlet top and nodded. *Definitely* for the best.

Especially when her eyes softened with spring-rain warmth. 'Damn, Finn. Do you still hurt that much?'

He realised then that she thought he didn't want to tackle the stairs.

'I—' He pulled in a breath. He *didn't* want to tackle the stairs. He'd overdone it today. He didn't want her to keep looking at him like that either, though. 'It's nothing a good night's sleep won't fix.'

Without another word, she strode to the room behind the kitchen and lifted his bag up onto the desk in there. So he wouldn't have to lift it himself later. Her thoughtfulness touched him. She could be prickly, and she could be mouthy, but she'd never been unkind.

Which was the reason, if he ever ran into Thomas Farquhar, he'd wring the mongrel's neck.

'Do you need anything else?'

The beds in Rupert's villa were always made up. He employed a cleaner to come in once a week so that the Russel siblings or any close friends could land here and fall into bed with a minimum of fuss. But even if the bed hadn't been made pride would've forbidden him from asking her to make it...or to help him make it.

He fell into a chair and slanted her a grin—cocky, assured and full of teasing to hide his pain as he pulled his hiking boots off. 'Well, now, Squirt...' He lifted a foot in her direction. 'I could use some help getting my socks off. And then maybe my jeans.'

As anticipated, her eyes went wide and her

cheeks went pink. Without another word, she whirled around and strode from the room.

At that precise moment his phone started to ring. He glanced at the caller ID and grimaced. 'Rupert, mate. Sorry about—'

The phone was summarily taken from him and Finn blinked when Audra lifted it to her ear. Up this close she smelled of coconut and peaches. His mouth watered. Dinner suddenly seemed like hours ago.

'Rupe, Finn looks like death. He needs to rest. He'll call you in the morning and you can give him an ear-bashing then.' She turned the phone off before handing it back to him. 'Goodnight, Finn.'

She was halfway through the kitchen before he managed to call back a goodnight of his own. He stood in the doorway and waited until he heard her ascending the stairs before closing his door and dialling Rupert's number.

'Before you launch into a tirade and tell me what an idiot I am, let me apologise. I'm calling myself far worse names than you ever will. I'd have not scared Audra for the world. I was going to call you in the morning to let you know I was here.' He'd had no notion Audra would be here.

It was a little early in the season for any of the Russels to head for the island.

Rupert's long sigh came down the phone, and it made Finn's gut churn. 'What are you doing in Kyanós?' his friend finally asked. 'I thought you were in Nice.'

'The, uh, cast came off yesterday.'

'And you couldn't blow off steam on the French Riviera?'

He scrubbed a hand down his face. 'There's a woman I'm trying to avoid and—'

'You don't need to say any more. I get the picture.'

Actually, Rupert was wrong. This time. It wasn't a romantic liaison he'd tired of and was fleeing. But he kept his mouth shut. He deserved Rupert's derision. 'If you want me to leave, I'll clear out at first light.'

His heart gave a sick kick at the long pause on the other end of the phone. Rupert was considering it! Rupert was the one person who'd shown faith in him when everyone else had written him off, and now—

'Of course I don't want you to leave.'

He closed his eyes and let out a long, slow breath.

'But…'

His eyes crashed open. His heart started to thud. 'But?'

'Don't go letting Audra fall in love with you. She's fragile at the moment, Finn…vulnerable.'

He stiffened. 'Whoa, Rupe! I've no designs on your little sister.'

'She's *exactly* your type.'

'Except she's your sister.' He made a decision then and there to leave in the morning. He didn't want Rupert worrying about this. It was completely unnecessary. He needed to lie low for a few weeks and Kyanós had seemed like the perfect solution, but not at the expense of either Rupert's or Audra's peace of mind.

'That said, I'm glad you're there.'

Finn stilled.

'I'm worried about her being on her own. I've been trying to juggle my timetable, but the earliest I can get away is in a fortnight.'

Finn pursed his lips. 'You want me to keep an eye on her?'

Again there was a long pause. 'She needs a bit of fun. She needs to let her hair down.'

'This *is* Audra we're talking about.' She was the most buttoned-up person he knew.

'You're good at fun.'

His lips twisted. He ought to be. He'd spent

a lifetime perfecting it. 'You want me to make sure she has a proper holiday?'

'Minus the holiday romance. Women *like* you, Finn…they fall for you.'

'Pot and kettle,' he grunted back. 'But you're worrying for nothing. Audra has more sense than that.' She had *always* disapproved of him and what she saw as his irresponsible and daredevil lifestyle.

What had happened eight weeks ago proved her point. What if the next time he did kill himself? The thought made his mouth dry and his gut churn. His body was recovering but his mind… There were days when he was a maelstrom of confusion, questioning the choices he was making. He gritted his teeth. It'd pass. After such a close brush with mortality it had to be normal to question one's life. Needless to say, he wasn't bringing anyone into that mess at the moment, especially not one who was his best friend's little sister.

'If she had more sense she'd have not fallen for Farquhar.'

Finn's hands fisted. 'Tell me the guy is toast.'

'I'm working on it.'

Good.

'I've tried to shield her from the worst of the media furore, but...'

'But she has eyes in her head. She can read the headlines for herself.' And those headlines had been everywhere. It'd been smart of Rupert to pack Audra off to the island.

'Exactly.' Rupert paused again. 'None of the Russels have any sense when it comes to love. If we did, Audra wouldn't have been taken in like she was.'

And she was paying for it now. He recalled her pallor, the dark circles beneath her eyes...the effort it'd taken her to lift his backpack. He could help with some of that—get her out into the sun, challenge her to swimming contests...and maybe even get her to run with him. He could make sure she ate three square meals a day.

'If I'd had more sense I'd have not fallen for Brooke Manning.'

'Everyone makes a bad romantic decision at least once in their lives, Rupe.'

He realised he sounded as if he were downplaying what had happened to his friend, and he didn't want to do that. Rupert hadn't looked at women in the same way after Brooke. Finn wasn't sure what had happened between them. He'd been certain they were heading for matrimony, babies and white picket fences. But it had all imploded, and Rupert hadn't been the same since. 'But you're right—not everyone gets their heart shredded.' He rubbed a hand across his chest. 'Has Farquhar shredded her heart?'

'I don't know.'

Even if he hadn't, he'd stolen company secrets from the Russel Corporation while posing as her attentive and very loving boyfriend. That wasn't something a woman like Audra would be able to shrug off as just a bad experience.

Poor Squirt.

He only realised he'd said that out loud when Rupert said with a voice as dry as a good single malt, 'Take a look, Finn. I think you'll find Squirt is all grown up.'

He didn't need to look. The less looking he did, the better. A girl like Audra deserved more than what a guy like him could give her—things like stability, peace of mind, and someone she could depend on.

'It'd be great if you could take her mind off things—make her laugh and have some fun. I just don't want her falling for you. She's bruised and battered enough.'

'You've nothing to worry about on that score,

Rupe, I promise you. I've no intention of hurting Audra. Ever.'

'She's special, Finn.'

That made him smile. 'All of the Russel siblings are special.'

'She's more selfless than the rest of us put together.'

Finn blinked. 'That's a big call.'

'It's the truth.'

He hauled in a breath and let it out slowly. 'I'll see what I can do.'

'Thanks, Finn, I knew I could count on you.'

Audra pressed her ringing phone to her ear at exactly eight twenty-three the next morning. She knew the exact time because she was wondering when Finn would emerge. She'd started clock-watching—a sure sign of worry. Not that she had any intention of letting Rupert know she was worried. 'Hey, Rupe.'

He called to check on her every couple of days, which only fed her guilt. Last night's false alarm sent an extra surge of guilt slugging through her now. 'Sorry about last night's fuss. I take it the police rang to let you know what happened.'

'They did. And you've nothing to apologise

for. Wasn't your fault. In fact, I'm proud of the way you handled the situation.'

He was? Her shoulders went back.

'Not everyone would've thought that quickly on their feet. You did good.'

'Thanks, I… I'm relieved it was just Finn.' She flashed to the lines of strain that had bracketed Finn's mouth last night. 'Do you know how long he plans to stay?'

'No idea. Do you mind him being there? I can ask him to leave.'

'No, no—don't do that.' She already owed Rupert and the rest of her family too much. She didn't want to cause any further fuss. 'He wasn't looking too crash hot last night. I think he needs to take it easy for a bit.'

'You could be right, Squirt, and I hate to ask this of you…'

'Ask away.' She marvelled how her brother's *Squirt* could sound so different from Finn's. When Finn called her Squirt it made her tingle all over.

'No, forget about it. It doesn't matter. You've enough on your plate.'

She had nothing on her plate at the moment and they both knew it. 'Tell me what you were going to say,' she ordered in her best boardroom voice. 'I insist. You know you'll get no peace now until you do.'

His low chuckle was her reward. Good. She wanted him to stop worrying about her.

'Okay, it's just… I'm a bit worried about him.'

She sat back. 'About Finn?' It made a change from Rupert worrying about her.

'He's never had to take it easy in his life. Going slow is an alien concept to him.'

He could say that again.

'He nearly died up there on that mountain.'

Her heart clenched. 'Died? I mean, I knew he'd banged himself up pretty bad, but… I had no idea.'

'Typical Finn, he's tried to downplay it. While the medical team could patch the broken arm and ribs easily enough, along with the dislocated shoulder and wrenched knee, his ruptured spleen and the internal bleeding nearly did him in.'

She closed her eyes and swallowed. 'You want me to make sure he takes it easy while he's here?'

'That's probably an impossible task.'

'Nothing's impossible,' she said with a confidence she had no right to. After all her brother's support these last few weeks—his lack of blame—she could certainly do this one thing for him. 'Consider it done.'

'And, Audra...?'

'Yes?'

'Don't go falling in love with him.'

She shot to her feet, her back ramrod straight. 'I make one mistake and—'

'This has nothing to do with what happened with Farquhar. It's just that women seem to like Finn. *A lot.* They fall at his feet in embarrassing numbers.'

She snorted and took her seat again. 'That's because he's pretty.' She preferred a man with a bit more substance.

You thought Thomas had substance.

She pushed the thought away.

'He's in Kyanós partly because he's trying to avoid some woman in Nice.'

Good to know.

'If he hurts you, Squirt, I'll no longer consider him a friend.'

She straightened from her slouch, air whistling between her teeth. Rupert and Finn were best friends, and had been ever since they'd attended their international boarding school in Geneva as fresh-faced twelve-year-olds.

She made herself swallow. 'I've no intention of doing anything so daft.' She'd never do anything to ruin her brother's most important friendship.

'Finn has a brilliant mind, he's built a successful company and is an amazing guy, but…'

'But what?' She frowned, when her brother remained silent. 'What are you worried about?'

'His past holds him back.'

By *his past* she guessed he meant Finn's parents' high-octane lifestyle, followed by their untimely deaths. It had to have had an impact on Finn, had to have left scars and wounds that would never heal.

'I worry he could end up like his father.'

She had to swallow the bile that rose through her.

'I'm not sure he'll ever settle down.'

She'd worked that much out for herself. And she wasn't a masochist. Men like Finn were pretty to look at, but you didn't build a life around them.

Women had flings with men like Finn…and she suspected they enjoyed every moment of them. A squirrel of curiosity wriggled through her, but she ruthlessly cut it off. One disastrous romantic liaison was enough for the year. She wasn't adding another one to the tally. She suppressed a shudder. The very thought made her want to crawl back into bed and pull the covers over her head.

She forced her spine to straighten. She had no

intention of falling for Finn, but she could get him to slow down for a bit—just for a week or two, right?

CHAPTER TWO

'YOU HAD BREAKFAST YET, Squirt?'

Audra almost jumped out of her skin at the deep male voice and the hard-muscled body that materialised directly in front of her. She bit back a yelp and pressed a hand to her heart. After sitting here waiting for him to emerge, she couldn't believe she'd been taken off guard.

He chuckled. 'You never used to be jumpy.'

Yeah, well, that was before Thomas Farquhar had locked her in a cupboard. The laughter in his warm brown eyes faded as they narrowed. Not that she had any intention of telling him that. She didn't want his pity. 'Broken sleep never leaves me at my best,' she said in as tart a voice as she could muster. Which was, admittedly, pretty tart.

He just grinned. 'I find it depends on the reasons for the broken sleep.' And then he sent her a broad wink.

She rolled her eyes. 'Glass shattering and having to call the police doesn't fall into the fun category, Finn.'

'Do you want me to apologise again? Do the full grovel?' He waggled his eyebrows. 'I'm very good at a comprehensive grovel.'

'No, thank you.' She pressed her lips together. She bet he was good at a lot of things.

She realised she still held her phone. She recalled the conversation she'd just had with Rupert and set it to the table, heat flushing through her cheeks.

Finn glanced at her and at the phone before cracking eggs into the waiting frying pan. 'So... Rupe rang to warn you off, huh?'

Her jaw dropped. How on earth...? *Ah.* 'He rang you too.'

'You want a couple of these?' He lifted an egg in her direction.

'No...thank you,' she added as a belated afterthought. It struck her that she always found it hard to remember her manners around Finn.

'Technically, I called him.' The frying pan spat and sizzled. 'But he seems to think I have some magic ability to make women swoon at my feet, whereby I pick them off at my leisure and have my wicked way with them before discarding them as is my wont.'

She frowned. Had she imagined the bitterness behind the lightness?

'He read me the Riot Act where you're concerned.' He sent her a mock serious look. 'So, Squirt, while I know it'll be hard for you to contain your disappointment, I'm afraid I'm not allowed to let a single one of my love rays loose in your direction.'

She couldn't help it, his nonsense made her laugh.

With an answering grin, he set a plate of eggs and toast in front of her and slid into the seat opposite.

'But I said I didn't want any.'

Her stomach rumbled, making a liar of her. Rather than tease her, though, he shrugged. 'Sorry, I must've misheard.'

Finn never misheard anything, but the smell of butter on toast made her mouth water. She picked up her knife and fork. It'd be wasteful not to eat it. 'Did Rupert order you to feed me up?' she grumbled.

He shook his head, and shaggy hair—damp from the shower—fell into his eyes and curled about his neck and some pulse inside her flared to life before she brutally strangled it.

'Nope. Rupe's only dictum was to keep my

love rays well and truly away from his little sister. All uttered in his most stern of tones.'

She did her best not to choke on her toast and eggs. 'Doesn't Rupert know me at all?' She tossed the words back at him with what she hoped was a matching carelessness.

'See? That's what I told him. I said, Audra's too smart to fall for a guy like me.'

Fall for? Absolutely not. Sleep with…?

What on earth…? She frowned and forced the thought away. She didn't think of Finn in those terms.

Really?

She rolled her shoulders. So what if she'd always thought him too good-looking for his own good? That didn't mean anything. In idle moments she might find herself thinking he'd be an exciting lover. If she were the kind of person who did flings with devil-may-care men. But she wasn't. And *that* didn't mean anything either.

'So…?'

She glanced up at the question in his voice.

'How long have you been down here?'

'Two days.'

'And how long are you here for?'

She didn't really know. 'A fortnight, maybe. I've taken some annual leave.'

He sent her a sharp glance from beneath brows so perfectly shaped they made her the tiniest bit jealous. 'If you took all the leave accrued by you, I bet you could stay here until the middle of next year.'

Which would be heaven—absolute heaven.

'What about you? How long are you staying?'

'I was thinking a week or two. Do some training…get some condition back.'

He was going to overdo it. Well, not on her watch!

'But if my being here is intruding on your privacy, I can shoot off to my uncle's place.'

'No need for that. It'll be nice to have some company.'

His eyes narrowed and she realised she'd overplayed her hand. It wasn't her usual sentiment where Finn was concerned. Normally she acted utterly disdainful and scornful. They sparred. They didn't buddy up.

She lifted her fork and pointed it at him. 'As long as you stop calling me Squirt, stop blathering nonsense about love rays…and cook me breakfast every day.'

He laughed and she let out a slow breath.

'You've got yourself a deal… *Audra*.'

Her name slid off his tongue like warm honey

and it was all she could do not to groan. She set her knife and fork down and pushed her plate away.

'I had no idea you didn't like being called Squirt.'

She didn't. Not really.

He stared at her for a moment. 'Don't hold Rupert's protectiveness against him.'

She blinked. 'I don't.' And then grimaced. 'Well, not much. I know I'm lucky to have him… and Cora and Justin.' It was a shame that Finn didn't have a brother or sister. He did have Rupert, though, and the two men were as close as brothers.

'He's a romantic.'

That made her glance up. 'Rupert?'

'Absolutely.'

He nodded and it made his hair do that fall-in-his-eyes thing again and she didn't know why, but it made her stomach clench.

'On the outside he acts as hard as nails, but on the inside…'

'He's a big marshmallow,' she finished.

'He'd go to the ends of the earth for someone he loved.'

That was true. She nodded.

'See? A romantic.'

She'd never thought about it in those terms.

His phone on the table buzzed. She didn't mean to look, but she saw the name Trixie flash up on the screen before Finn reached over and switched it off. *Okay.*

'So…' He dusted off his hands as if ready to take on the world. 'What were you planning to do while you were here?'

Dear God. *Think of nice, easy, relaxing things.* 'Um… I was going to lie on the beach and catch some rays—' *not love rays* '—float about in the sea for a bit.'

'Sounds good.'

Except he wouldn't be content with lying around and floating, would he? He'd probably challenge himself to fifty laps out to the buoy and back every day. 'Read a book.'

His lip curled. 'Read a book?'

She tried not to wince at the scorn that threaded through his voice.

'You come to one of the most beautiful places on earth to *read a book*?'

She tried to stop her shoulders from inching up to her ears. 'I like reading, and do you know how long it's been since I read a book for pleasure?'

'How long?'

'Over a year,' she mumbled.

He spread his hands. 'If you like to read, why don't you do more of it?'

Because she'd been working too hard. Because she'd let Thomas distract and manipulate her.

'And what else?'

She searched her mind. 'I don't cook.'

He glanced at their now empty plates and one corner of his mouth hooked up. 'So I've noticed.'

'But I want to learn to cook…um…croissants.'

His brow furrowed. 'Why?'

Because they took a long time to make, didn't they? The pastry needed lots of rolling out, didn't it? Which meant, if she could trick him into helping her, he'd be safe from harm while he was rolling out pastry. 'Because I love them.' That was true enough. 'But I've had to be strict with myself.'

'Strict, how?'

'I've made a decision—in the interests of both my waistline and my heart health—that I'm only allowed to eat croissants that I make myself.'

He leaned back and let loose with a long low whistle. 'Wow, Squ— Audra! You really know how to let your hair down and party, huh?'

No one in all her life had ever accused her of being a party animal.

'A holiday with reading and baking at the top of your list.'

His expression left her in no doubt what he thought about that. 'This is supposed to be a holiday—some R & R,' she shot back, stung. 'I'm all go, go, go at work, but here I want time out.'

'Boring,' he sing-songed.

'Relaxing,' she countered.

'You've left the recreation part out of your R & R equation. I mean, look at you. You even look…'

She had to clamp her hands around the seat of her chair to stop from leaping out of it. 'Boring?' she said through gritted teeth.

'Buttoned-up. Tense. The opposite of relaxed.'

'It's the effect you and your love rays always seem to have on me.'

He tsk-tsked and shook his head. 'We're not supposed to mention the love rays, remember?'

Could she scream yet?

'I mean, look at your hair. You have it pulled back *in a bun*.'

She touched a hand to her hair. 'What's wrong with that?'

'A bun is for the boardroom, not the beach.'

She hated wearing her hair down and have it tickle her face.

'Well, speaking of hair, you might want to visit a hairdresser yourself when you're next in the village,' she shot back.

'But I visited my hairdresser only last week.' He sent her a grin full of wickedness and sin. 'The delectable Monique assured me this look is all the rage at the moment.'

He had a hairdresser called Monique...who was delectable? She managed to roll her eyes. 'The *too-long-for-the-boardroom-just-right-for-the-beach* look?'

'Precisely. She said the same about the stubble.'

She'd been doing her best not to notice that stubble. She was trying to keep the words *dead sexy* from forming in her brain.

'What do you think?' He ran a hand across his jawline, preening. It should've made him look ridiculous. Especially as he was hamming it up and trying to look ridiculous. But she found herself having to jam down on the temptation to reach across and brush her palm across it to see if it was as soft and springy as it looked.

She mentally slapped herself. 'I think it looks... scruffy.' In the best possible way. 'But it probably provides good protection against the sun, which is wise in these climes.'

He simply threw his head back and laughed, not taking the slightest offence. The strain that had deepened the lines around his eyes last night had eased. And when he rose to take their dishes to the sink he moved with an easy fluidity that belied his recent injuries.

He almost died up there on that mountain.

She went cold all over.

'Audra?'

She glanced up to find him staring at her, concern in his eyes. She shook herself. 'What's your definition of a good holiday, then?'

'Here on the island?'

He'd started to wash the dishes so she rose to dry them. 'Uh-huh, here on the island.'

'Water sports,' he said with relish.

'What kind of water sports?' Swimming and kayaking were gentle enough, but—

'On the other side of the island is the most perfect cove for windsurfing and sailing.'

But…but he could hurt himself.

'Throw in some water-skiing and hang-gliding and I'd call that just about the perfect holiday.'

He could kill himself! Lord, try explaining *that* to Rupert. 'No way.'

He glanced at her. 'When did you become such a scaredy-cat, Audra Russel?'

She realised he thought her 'No way' had been in relation to herself, which was just as well because if he realised she'd meant it for him he'd immediately go out and throw himself off the first cliff he came across simply to spite her.

And while it might be satisfying to say I told you so if he did come to grief, she had a feeling that satisfaction would be severely tempered if the words were uttered in a hospital ward...or worse.

'Why don't you let your hair down for once, take a risk? You might even find it's fun.'

She bit back a sigh. Maybe that was what she was afraid of. One risk could lead to another, and before she knew it she could've turned her whole life upside down. And she wasn't talking sex with her brother's best friend here either. Which—*obviously*—wasn't going to happen. She was talking about her job and her whole life. It seemed smarter to keep a tight rein on all her risk-taking impulses. She was sensible, stable and a rock to all her family. That was *who* she was. She repeated the words over and over like a mantra until she'd fixed them firmly in her mind again.

She racked her brain to think of a way to control Finn's risk-taking impulses too. 'There's absolutely nothing wrong with some lazy R & R, Finn Sullivan.' She used his full name in the same way he'd used hers. 'You should try it some time.'

His eyes suddenly gleamed. 'I'll make a deal with you. I'll try your kind of holiday R & R if you'll try mine?'

She bit her lip, her pulse quickening. This could be the perfect solution. 'So you'd be prepared to laze around here with a book if I…if I try windsurfing and stuff?'

'Yep. Quid pro quo.'

'Meaning?'

'One day we do whatever you choose. The next day we do whatever I choose.'

She turned to hang up the tea towel so he couldn't see the self-satisfied smile that stretched across her face. For at least half of his stay she'd be able to keep him out of trouble. As for the other half…she could temper his pace—be so inept he'd have to slow down to let her keep up or have to spend so much time teaching her that there'd been no time for him to be off risking his own neck. *Perfect.*

She swung back. 'Despite what you say, I'm not a scaredy-cat.'

'And despite what you think, I'm not hyper-active.'

Finn held his breath as he watched Audra weigh up his suggestion. She was actually consider-ing it. Which was surprising. He'd expected her to tell him to take a flying leap and stalk off to read her book.

But she was actually considering his sugges-tion and he didn't know why. He thought he'd need to tease and rile her more, bring her latent competitive streak to the fore, where she'd ac-cept his challenge simply to save face. Still, he *had* tossed out the bait of her proving that her way was better than his. Women were always trying to change him. Maybe Audra found that idea attractive too?

In the next moment he shook his head. That'd only be the case if she were interested in him as a romantic prospect. And she'd made it clear that wasn't the case.

Thank God.

He eyed that tight little bun and swallowed.

'I'll agree to your challenge…'

He tried to hide his surprise. She would? He hadn't even needed to press her.

'On two conditions.'

Ha! He knew it couldn't be that easy. 'Which are?'

'I get to go first.'

He made a low sweeping bow. 'Of course— ladies first, that always went without saying.' It was a minor concession and, given how much he still hurt, one he didn't mind making. They could pick up the pace tomorrow.

'And the challenge doesn't start until tomorrow.'

He opened his mouth to protest, but she forged on. 'We need to go shopping. There's hardly any food in the place. And I'm not wasting my choice of activities on practicalities like grocery shopping, thank you very much.'

'We could get groceries delivered.'

'But it'd be nice to check out the produce at the local market. Rupert likes to support the local businesses.'

And while she was here she'd consider herself Rupert's representative. And it was true—what she did here would reflect on her brother. The

Russels had become a bit of a fixture in Kyanós life over the last few years.

'I also want to have a deliciously long browse in the bookstore. And you'll need to select a book too, you know?'

Oh, joy of joys. He was going to make her run two miles for that.

'And...' she shrugged '...consider it a fact-finding mission—we can research what the island has to offer and put an itinerary together.'

Was she really going to let him choose half of her holiday activities for the next week or two? *Excellent.* By the time he was through with her, she'd have colour in her cheeks, skin on her bones—not to mention some muscle tone and a spring in her step. 'You've got yourself a deal... on one condition.'

Her eyebrows lifted.

'That you lose the bun.' He couldn't think straight around that bun. Whenever he glanced at it, he was seized by an unholy impulse to release it. It distracted him beyond anything.

Without another word, she reached up to pull the pins from her bun, and a soft cloud of fair hair fell down around her shoulders. Her eyes narrowed and she thrust out her chin. 'Better?'

It took an effort of will to keep a frown from his face. A tight band clamped around his chest.

'Is it *beachy* enough for you?'

'A hundred per cent better,' he managed, fighting the urge to reach out and touch a strand, just to see if it was as silky and soft as it looked.

She smirked and pulled it back into a ponytail. 'There, the bun is gone.'

But the ponytail didn't ease the tightness growing in his chest, not to mention other places either. It bounced with a perky insolence that had him aching to reach out and give it a gentle tug. For pity's sake, it was just hair!

She stilled, and then her hands went to her hips. 'Are you feeling okay, Finn?'

He shook himself. 'Of course I am. Why?'

'You gave in to my conditions without a fight. That's not like you. Normally you'd bicker with me and angle for more.'

Damn! He had to remember how quick she was, and keep his wits about him.

'If you want a few more days before embarking on our challenge, that's fine with me. I mean, you only just got the cast off your arm.'

He clenched his jaw so hard it started to ache.

'I understand you beat yourself up pretty bad on that mountain.'

She paused as if waiting for him to confirm that, but he had no intention of talking about his accident.

She shrugged. 'And you looked pretty rough last night so…'

'So…what?'

'So if you needed a couple of days to re-group…'

Anger directed solely at himself pooled in his stomach. 'The accident was two month ago, *Squirt.*' He called her Squirt deliberately, to set her teeth on edge. 'I'm perfectly fine.'

She shrugged. 'Whatever you say.' But she didn't look convinced. 'I'm leaving for the village in half an hour if you want to come along. But if you want to stay here and do push-ups and run ten miles on the beach then I'm more than happy to select a book for you.'

'Not a chance.' He shuddered to think what she would make him read as a penance. 'I'll be ready in twenty.'

'Suit yourself.' She moved towards the foyer and the stairs. And the whole time her ponytail swayed in jaunty mockery. She turned when she reached the foyer's archway. 'Finn?'

He hoped to God she hadn't caught him staring. 'What?'

'The name's Audra, not Squirt. That was the deal. Three strikes and you're out. That's Strike One.'

She'd kick him out if he… He stared after her and found himself grinning. She wasn't going to let him push her around and he admired her for it.

'I'll drive,' Finn said, thirty minutes later.

'I have the car keys,' Audra countered, sliding into the driver's seat of the hybrid Rupert kept on the island for running back and forth to the village.

To be perfectly honest, he didn't care who drove. He just didn't want Audra to think him frail or in need of babying. Besides, it was only ten minutes into the village.

One advantage of being passenger, though, was the unencumbered opportunity to admire the views, and out here on the peninsula the views were spectacular. Olive trees interspersed with the odd cypress and ironwood tree ranged down the slopes, along with small scrubby shrubs bursting with flowers—some white and some pink. And beyond it all was the unbelievable, almost magical blue of the Aegean Sea. The air from the open windows was warm and dry, fragrant with salt and rosemary, and something inside him started to unhitch. He rested his head back and breathed it all in.

'Glorious, isn't it?'

He glanced across at her profile. She didn't drive as if she needed to be anywhere in a hurry. Her fingers held the steering wheel in a loose, relaxed grip, and the skin around her eyes and mouth was smooth and unblemished. The last time he'd seen her she'd been in a rush, her knuckles white around her briefcase and her eyes narrowed—no doubt her mind focussed on the million things on her to-do list.

She glanced across. 'What?'

'I was just thinking how island life suits you.'

Her brows shot up, and she fixed her attention on the road in front again, her lips twitching. 'Wow, you must really hate my bun.'

No, he loved that bun.

Not that he had any intention of telling her that.

She flicked him with another of her cool glances. 'Do you know anyone that this island life wouldn't suit?'

'Me...in the long term. I'd go stir-crazy after a while.' He wasn't interested in holidaying his whole life away.

What are you interested in doing with the rest of your life, then?

He swallowed and shoved the question away, not ready to face the turmoil it induced, focussed his attention back on Audra.

'And probably you too,' he continued. 'Seems to me you don't like being away from the office for too long.'

Something in her tensed, though her fingers still remained loose and easy on the wheel. He wanted to turn more fully towards her and study her to find out exactly what had changed, but she'd challenge such a stare, and he couldn't think of an excuse that wouldn't put her on the defensive. Getting her to relax and have fun was the remit, not making her tense and edgy. His mention of work had probably just been an unwelcome reminder of Farquhar.

And it was clear she wanted to talk about Farquhar as much as he wanted to talk about his accident.

He cleared his throat. 'But in terms of a short break, I don't think anything can beat this island.'

'Funnily enough, that's one argument you won't get from me.'

He didn't know why, but her words made him laugh.

They descended into the village and her sigh of appreciation burrowed into his chest. 'It's such a pretty harbour.'

She steered the car down the narrow street to the parking area in front of the harbour wall. They sat for a moment to admire the scene spread before them. An old-fashioned ferry chugged out of the cove, taking passengers on the two-hour ride to the mainland. Yachts with brightly coloured sails bobbed on their moorings. The local golden stone of the harbour wall provided the perfect foil for the deep blue of the water. To their left houses in the same golden stone, some of them plastered brilliant white, marched up the hillside, the bright blue of their doors and shutters making the place look deliciously Mediterranean.

Audra finally pushed out of the car and he followed. She pulled her hair free of its band simply to capture it again, including the strand that had worked its way loose, and retied it. 'I was just going to amble along the main shopping strip for a bit.'

She gestured towards the cheerful curve of shops that lined the harbour, the bunting from their awnings fluttering in the breeze. Barrels of gaily coloured flowers stood along the strip at intervals. If there was a more idyllic place on earth, he was yet to find it.

'Sounds good to me.' While she was ambling she'd be getting a dose of sun and fresh air. 'Do you mind if I tag along?' He asked because he'd called her Squirt earlier to deliberately rub her up the wrong way and he regretted it now.

Cool blue eyes surveyed him and he couldn't read them at all. 'I mean to take my time. I won't be rushed. I do enough rushing in my real life and...'

Her words trailed off and he realised she thought he meant to whisk her through the shopping at speed and...and what? Get to the things he wanted to do? What kind of selfish brute did she think he was? 'I'm in no rush.'

'I was going to browse the markets and shops... maybe get some lunch, before buying whatever groceries we needed before heading back.'

'Sounds like an excellent plan.'

The faintest of frowns marred the perfect skin of her forehead. 'It does?'

Something vulnerable passed across her features, but it was gone in a flash. From out of nowhere Rupert's words came back to him: *She's*

more selfless than the rest of us put together.'
The Russel family came from a privileged background, but they took the associated social responsibility of that position seriously. Each of them had highly honed social consciences. But it struck him then that Audra put her family's needs before her own. Who put her needs first?

'Audra, a lazy amble along the harbour, while feeling the sun on my face and breathing in the sea air, sounds pretty darn perfect to me.'

She smiled then—a real smile—and it kicked him in the gut because it was so beautiful. And because he realised he'd so very rarely seen her smile like that.

Why?

He took her arm and led her across the street, releasing her the moment they reached the other side. She still smelled of coconut and peaches, and it made him want to lick her.

Dangerous.

Not to mention totally inappropriate.

He tried to find his equilibrium again, and for once wished he could blame his sense of vertigo, the feeling of the ground shifting beneath his feet, on his recent injuries. Audra had always been able to needle him and then make him laugh, but he had no intention of letting her get under his skin. Not in *that* way. He'd been out of circulation too long, that was all. He'd be fine again once he'd regained his strength and put the accident behind him.

'It's always so cheerful down here,' she said, pausing beside one of the flower-filled barrels, and dragging a deep breath into her lungs.

He glanced down at the flowers to avoid noticing the way her chest lifted, and touched his fingers to a bright pink petal. 'These are…nice.'

'I love petunias,' she said. She touched a scarlet blossom. 'And these geraniums and begonias look beautiful.'

He reached for a delicate spray of tiny white flowers at the same time that she did, and their fingers brushed against each other. It was the briefest of contacts, but it sent electricity charging up his arm and had him sucking in a breath. For one utterly unbalancing moment he thought she meant to repeat the gesture.

'That's alyssum,' she said, pulling her hand away.

He moistened his lips. 'I had no idea you liked gardening.'

She stared at him for a moment and he watched her snap back into herself like a rubber band that had been stretched and then released. But opposite to that because the stretching had seemed to relax her while the snapping back had her all tense again.

'Don't worry, Finn. I'm not going to make you garden while you're here.'

Something sad and hungry, though, lurked in the backs of her eyes, and he didn't understand it at all. He opened his mouth to ask her about it, but closed it again. He didn't get involved with complicated emotions or sensitive issues. He avoided them like the plague. Get her to laugh, get her to loosen up. That was his remit. Nothing more. But that didn't stop the memory of that sad and hungry expression from playing over and over in his mind.

CHAPTER THREE

AUDRA WHEELED AWAY from Finn and the barrel of flowers to survey the length of the village street, and tried to slow the racing of her pulse…to quell the temptation that swept through her like the breeze tugging at her hair. But the sound of the waves splashing against the seawall and the sparkles of light on the water as the sun danced off its surface only fed the yearning and the restlessness.

She couldn't believe that the idea—the temptation—had even occurred to her. She and Finn? The idea was laughable.

For pity's sake, she'd had one romantic disaster this year. Did she really want to follow that up with another?

Absolutely not.

She dragged a trembling hand across her eyes. She must be more shaken by Thomas and his betrayal than she'd realised. She needed to focus on herself and her family, and to make things right again. That was what this break here on

Kyanós was all about—that and avoiding the media storm that had surrounded her in Geneva. The one thing she didn't want to do was to make things worse.

The building at the end of the row of shops drew her gaze. Its white walls and blue shutters gleamed in the sun like the quintessential advertisement for a Greek holiday. The For Sale sign made her swallow. She resolutely dragged her gaze away, but the gaily coloured planter pots dotted along the thoroughfare caught her gaze again and that didn't help either. But...

A sigh welled inside her. But if she ever owned a shop, she'd have a tub—or maybe two tubs—of flowers like these outside its door.

You're never going to own a shop.

She made herself straighten. No, she was never going to own a shop. And the sooner she got over it, the better.

The lengthening silence between her and Finn grew more and more fraught.

See what happens when you don't keep a lid on the nonsense? You become tempted to do ridiculous things.

Well, she could annihilate that in one fell swoop.

'If I ever owned a shop, I'd want flowers outside its door too, just like these ones.' And she waited for the raucous laughter to scald her dream with the scorn it deserved.

Rather than laughter a warm chuckle greeted her, a chuckle filled with…affection? 'You used to talk about opening a shop when you were a little girl.'

And everyone had laughed at her—teased her for not wanting to be something more glamorous like an astronaut or ballerina.

Poor poppet, she mocked herself.

'What did you want to be when you were little?'

'A fireman…a knife-thrower at the circus…an explorer…and I went through a phase of wanting to be in a glam-rock band. It was the costumes,' he added when she swung to stare at him. 'I loved the costumes.'

She couldn't help but laugh. 'I'm sure you'd look fetching in purple satin, platform boots and silver glitter.'

He snorted.

'You know what the next challenge is going to be, don't you? The very next fancy dress party you attend, you have to go as a glam rocker.'

'You know there'll be a counter challenge to that?'

'There always is.' And whatever it was, she wouldn't mind honouring it. She'd pay good money to see Finn dressed up like that.

One corner of his mouth had hooked up in a cocky grin, his eyes danced with devilment, and his hair did that 'slide across his forehead perilously close to his eyes' thing and her stomach clenched. Hard. She forced her gaze away, reminded herself who he was. And what he was. 'Well, it might not come with fancy costumes, but playboy adventurer captures the spirit of your childhood aspirations.'

He slanted a glance down at her, the laughter in his eyes turning dark and mocking, though she didn't know if it was directed at her or himself. 'Wow,' he drawled. 'Written off in one simple phrase. You've become a master of the back-handed compliment. Though some might call it character assassination.'

It was her turn to snort. 'While you've perfected drama queen.' But she found herself biting her lip as she stared unseeing at the nearby shop fronts as they walked along. Had she been too hard, too...*dismissive* just then? 'I'm not discounting the fact that you make a lot of money for charity.'

The car races, the mountaineering expeditions, the base jumps were all for terribly worthy causes.

'And yet she can't hide her disapproval at my reckless and irresponsible lifestyle,' he told the sky.

It wasn't disapproval, but envy. Not that she had any intention of telling him so. All right, there was some disapproval too. She didn't understand why he had to risk his neck for charity. There were other ways to fundraise, right? Risking his neck just seemed…stupid.

But whatever else Finn was, she'd never accuse him of being stupid.

She was also officially tired of this conversation. She halted outside the bookshop. 'Our first stop.'

She waited for him to protest but all he did was gesture for her to precede him. 'After you.'

With a big breath she entered, and crossed her fingers and hoped none of the shopkeepers or villagers would mention her recent troubles when they saw her today. She just wanted to forget all about that for a while.

They moved to different sections of the store—him to Non-Fiction, while she started towards Popular Fiction, stopping along the way to pore over the quaint merchandise that lined the front of the shop—cards and pens, bookmarks in every shape and size, some made from paper while others were made from bits of crocheted string with coloured beads dangling from their tails. A large selection of journals and notebooks greeted her too, followed by bookends and paperweights—everything a booklover could need. How she loved this stuff! On her way out she'd buy a gorgeous notebook. Oh, and bookmarks—one for each book she bought.

She lost herself to browsing the row upon row of books then; most were in Greek but some were in English too. She didn't know for how long she scanned titles, admired covers and read back-cover blurbs, but she slowly became aware of Finn watching her from where he sat on one of the low stools that were placed intermittently about the shop for customers' convenience. She surprised a look of affection on his face, and it made her feel bad for sniping at him earlier and dismissing him as a playboy adventurer.

He grinned. 'You look like you're having fun.'

'I am.' This slow browsing, the measured contemplation of the delights offered up on these shelves—the sheer *unrushedness* of it all—filled something inside her. She glanced at his hands, his lap, the floor at his feet. 'You don't have a book yet.'

He nodded at the stack she held. 'Are you getting all of those?'

'I'm getting the French cookbook.' She'd need a recipe for croissants. 'And three of these.'

He took the cookbook from her, and then she handed him two women's fiction titles and a cosy mystery, before putting the others back where they belonged.

'What would you choose for me?' His lip curled as he reached forward to flick a disparaging finger at a blockbuster novel from a big-name writer. 'Something like that?'

'That's a historical saga with lots of period detail. I'd have not thought it was your cup of tea at all.' She suspected the pace would be a bit slow for his taste. 'The object of the exercise isn't to make you suffer.'

Amber eyes darker than the whisky he liked but just as intoxicating swung to her and she saw the surprise in their depths. She recalled the affection she'd surprised in his face a moment ago and swallowed. Had she become a complete and utter shrew somewhere over the last year or two? 'I know that our modus operandi is to tease each other and…and to try to best each other—all in fun, of course.'

He inclined his head. 'Of course.'

'But I want to show you that quieter pursuits can be pleasurable too. If I were choosing a book for you I'd get you—' she strode along to the humour section '—this.' She pulled out a book by a popular comedian that she knew he liked.

He blinked and took it.

She set off down the next row of shelves. 'And to be on the safe side I'd get you this as well…or this.' She pulled out two recent non-fiction releases. One a biography of a well-known sportsman, and the other on World War Two.

He nodded towards the second one and she added it to the growing pile of books in his arms.

She started back the way they'd come. 'If I were on my own I'd get you this one as a joke.' She held up a self-help book with the title *Twelve Rules for Life: An Antidote to Chaos*.

'Put it back.'

The laughter in his voice added a spring to her step. She slotted it back into place. 'I'd get you a wildcard too.'

'A wildcard?'

'A book on spec—something you might not like, but could prove to be something you'd love.'

He pursed his lips for a moment and then nodded. 'I want a wildcard.'

Excellent. But what? She thought back over what he'd said earlier—about wanting to be a fireman, a knife-thrower, an explorer. She returned to the fiction shelves. She'd bet her house on the fact he'd love tales featuring heroic underdogs. She pulled a novel from the shelf—the first book in a fantasy trilogy from an acclaimed writer.

'That's...that's a doorstop!'

'Yes or no?'

He blew out a breath. 'What the hell, add it to the pile.'

She did, and then retrieved her own books from his arms. 'I'm not letting you buy my books.'

'Why not?'

'I like to buy my own books. And I've thrust three books onto you that you may never open.'

He stretched his neck, first one way and then the other. 'Can I buy you lunch?'

'As a thank you for being your bookstore personal shopper? Absolutely. But let's make it a late lunch. I'm still full from breakfast.'

She stopped to select her bookmarks, and added two notebooks to her purchases. Finn chose a bookmark of his own, and then seized a satchel in butter-soft black leather. 'Perfect.'

Perfect for what? She glanced at the selection of leather satchels and calico book bags and bit her lip. Maybe—

With a laugh, Finn propelled her towards the counter. 'Save them for your next visit.'

They paid and while Audra exchanged greetings with Sibyl, the bookshop proprietor, he put all their purchases into the satchel and slung it over his shoulder. 'Where to next?'

She stared at that bag. It'd make his shoulder ache if he wasn't careful. But then she realised it was on his right shoulder, not his left, and let out a breath. 'Wherever the mood takes us,' she said as they moved towards the door.

She paused to read the community announcement board and an advertisement for art classes jumped out at her. Oh, that'd be fun and...

She shook her head. R & R was all very well, but she had to keep herself contained to the beach and her books. Anything else... Well, anything else was just too hard. And she was too tired.

Finn trailed a finger across the flyer. 'Interested?'

She shook her head and led him outside.

He frowned at her. 'But—'

'Ooh, these look like fun.' She shot across to the boutique next door and was grateful when he let himself be distracted.

They flicked through a rack of discounted clothing that stood in blatant invitation out the front. Finn bought a pair of swimming trunks, so she added a sarong to her growing list of purchases. They browsed the markets. Finn bought a pair of silver cufflinks in the shape of fat little aeroplanes. 'My uncle will love these.' He pointed to an oddly shaped silver pendant on a string of black leather. 'That'd look great on you.' So she bought that too. They helped each other choose sunhats.

It felt decadent to be spending like this, not that any of her purchases were particularly pricey. But she so rarely let herself off the leash that she blithely ignored the voice of puritan sternness that tried to reel her in. What was more, it gave her the chance to exchange proper greetings with the villagers she'd known for years now.

Her worries she'd be grilled about Thomas and her reputed broken heart and the upcoming court case dissolved within ten minutes. As always, the people of Kyanós embraced her as if she were one of their own. And she loved them for it. The Russel family had been coming for holidays here for nearly ten years now. Kyanós felt like a home away from home.

'Hungry yet?'

'Famished!' She glanced at her watch and did a double take when she saw it was nearly two o'clock. 'We haven't done the bakery, the butcher, the delicatessen or the wine merchant yet.'

'We have time.'

She lifted her face to the sun and closed her eyes to relish it even more. 'We do.'

They chose a restaurant that had a terrace overlooking the harbour and ordered a shared platter of warm olives, cured meats and local cheeses accompanied with bread warm from the oven and a cold crisp carafe of *retsina*. While they ate they browsed their book purchases.

Audra surreptitiously watched Finn as he sampled the opening page of the fantasy novel…and then the next page…and the one after that.

He glanced up and caught her staring. He hesitated and then shrugged. 'You know, this might be halfway decent.'

She refrained from saying I told you so. 'Good.'

'If I hadn't seen you choose me those first two books I'd have not given this one a chance. I'd have written it off as a joke like the self-help book. And as I suspect I'll enjoy both these other books...'

If he stayed still long enough to read them.

He frowned.

She folded her arms. 'Why does that make you frown?'

'I'm wishing I'd known about this book when I was laid up in hospital with nothing to do.'

The shadows in his eyes told her how stir-crazy he'd gone. 'What did you do to pass the time?'

'Crosswords. And I watched lots of movies.'

'And chafed.'

'Pretty much.'

'I almost sent you a book, but I thought...'

'You thought I'd misinterpret the gesture? Think you were rubbing salt into the wound?'

Something like that.

He smiled. 'I appreciated the puzzle books.' And then he scowled. 'I didn't appreciate the grapes, though. Grapes are for invalids.'

She stiffened. 'It was supposed to be an entire basket of fruit!' Not just grapes.

'Whatever. I'd have preferred a bottle of tequila. I gave the fruit to the nurses.'

But his eyes danced as he feigned indignation and it was hard to contain a grin. 'I'll keep that in mind for next time.'

He gave a visible shudder and she grimaced in sympathy. 'Don't have a next time.' She raised her glass. 'To no more accidents and a full and speedy recovery.'

'I'll drink to that.'

He lifted his glass to hers and then sipped it with an abandoned enjoyment she envied. 'Who knew you'd be such fun to shop with?'

The words shot out of her impulsively, and she found herself speared on the end of a keen-edged glance. 'You thought I'd chafe?'

'A bit,' she conceded. 'I mean, Rupert and Justin will put up with it when Cora or I want to window-shop, but they don't enjoy it.'

'I wouldn't want to do it every day.'

Neither would she.

'But today has been fun.' He stared at her for a beat too long. 'It was a revelation watching you in the bookstore.'

She swallowed. Revelation, how?

'It's been a long time since I saw you enjoy yourself so much, Squirt, and—' He shot back in his seat. 'Audra! I meant to say Audra. Don't make that Strike Two. I...'

He gazed at her helplessly and she forgave him instantly. He hadn't said it to needle her the way he had with his earlier *Squirt*. She shook herself. 'Sorry, what were you saying? I was miles away.'

He smiled his thanks, but then leaned across the table towards her, and that smile and his closeness made her breath catch. 'You should do things you enjoy more often, Miss Conscientiousness.'

Hmm, she'd preferred Squirt.

'There's more to life than boardrooms and spreadsheets.'

'That's what holidays are for,' she agreed. The boardrooms and spreadsheets would be waiting for her at the end of it, though, and the thought made her feel tired to the soles of her feet.

CHAPTER FOUR

AUDRA GLANCED ACROSS at Finn, who looked utterly content lying on his towel on the sand of this ridiculously beautiful curve of beach, reading his book. It seemed ironic, then, that she couldn't lose herself in her own book.

She blamed it on the half-remembered dreams that'd given her a restless night. Scraps had been playing through her mind all morning—sexy times moving to the surreal and the scary; Finn's and Thomas's faces merging and then separating—leaving her feeling restless and strung tight.

One of those sexy-time moments played through her mind again now and she bit her lip against the warmth that wanted to spread through her. The fact that this beach was so ridiculously private didn't help. She didn't want the words *private* and *Finn*—or *sexy times*—to appear in the same thought with such tempting symmetry. It was *crazy*. She'd always done her best to not look at Finn in *that* way. And she had no intention of letting her guard down now.

This whole preoccupation was just a…a way for her subconscious to avoid focussing on what needed to be dealt with. Which was to regather her resources and refocus her determination to be of service at the Russel Corporation, to be a valuable team member rather than a liability.

'What was that sigh for?'

She blinked to find Finn's beautiful brown eyes surveying her. And they were beautiful—the colour of cinnamon and golden syrup and ginger beer, and fringed with long dark lashes. She didn't know how lashes could look decadent and sinful, but Finn's did.

'You're supposed to be relaxing—enjoying the sun and the sea…your book.'

'I am.'

'Liar.'

He rolled to his side to face her more fully, and she shrugged. 'I had a restless night.' She stifled a yawn. 'That's all.'

'When one works as hard as you do, it can be difficult to switch off.'

'Old habits,' she murmured, reaching for her T-shirt and pulling it over her head and then tying her sarong about her waist, feeling ridiculously naked in her modest one-piece.

Which was crazy because she and Finn and the

rest of her family had been on this beach countless times together, and in briefer swimsuits than what either of them were wearing now. 'I don't want to get too much sun all at once,' she said by way of explanation, although Finn hadn't indicated by so much as a blink of his gorgeous eyelashes that he'd wanted or needed one. She glanced at him. 'You've been incapacitated for a couple of months and yet I'm paler than you.'

'Yeah, but my incapacitation meant spending a lot of time on the rooftop terrace of my apartment on the French Riviera, so...not exactly doing it tough.'

Fair point.

'You ever tried meditation?'

'You're talking to me, Audra, remember?'

His slow grin raised all the tiny hairs on her arms. 'Lie on your back in a comfortable position and close your eyes.'

'Finn...' She could barely keep the whine out of her voice. 'Meditation makes me feel like a failure.' And there was more than enough of that in her life at the moment as it was, thank you very much. 'I know you're supposed to *clear your mind*, but...it's impossible!'

'Would you be so critical and hard on someone else? Cut yourself some slack.' He rolled onto his back. 'Work on quietening your mind rather than clearing it. When a thought appears, as it will, simply acknowledge it before focussing on your breathing again.'

He closed his eyes and waited. With another sigh, Audra rolled onto her back and settled her hat over her face. It was spring and the sun wasn't fierce, but she wasn't taking any chances. 'Okay,' she grumbled. 'I'm ready. What am I supposed to do?'

Finn led her through a guided meditation where she counted breaths, where she tensed and then relaxed different muscle groups. The deep timbre of his voice, unhurried and undemanding, soothed her in a way she'd have never guessed possible. Her mind wandered, as he'd said it would, but she brought her attention back to his voice and her breathing each time, and by the time he finished she felt weightless and light.

She heard no movement from him, so she stayed exactly where she was—on a cloud of euphoric relaxation.

And promptly fell asleep.

Finn didn't move until Audra's deep rhythmic breaths informed him that she was asleep. Not a light and sweet little nap, but fully and deeply asleep.

He rolled onto his tummy and rested his chin on his arms. When had she forgotten how to relax? He'd spent a large portion of every Christmas vacation from the age of twelve onwards with the Russel family.

She'd been a sweet, sparky little kid, fiercely determined to keep up with her older siblings and not be left behind. As a teenager she'd been curious, engaged...and a bit more of a dreamer than the others, not as driven in a particular direction as they'd been either. But then he'd figured that'd made her more of an all-rounder.

When had she lost her zest, her joy for life? During her final years of school? At university? He swallowed. When her mother had died?

Karen Russel had died suddenly of a cerebral aneurysm ten years ago. It'd shattered the entire family. Audra had only been seventeen.

Was it then that Audra had exchanged her joy in life for...? For what? To become a workaholic managing the charitable arm of her family's corporation? In her grief, had she turned away from the things that had given her joy? Had it become a habit?

He recalled the odd defiance in her eyes when

she'd spoken about owning a shop—the way she'd mocked the idea…and the way the mockery and defiance had been at odds. He turned to stare at her. 'Hell, sweetheart,' he whispered. 'What are you doing to yourself?'

She slept for an hour, and Finn was careful to pretend not to notice when she woke, even though his every sense was honed to her every movement. He kept his nose buried in his book and feigned oblivion, which wasn't that hard because the book was pretty gripping.

'Hey,' she said in sleepy greeting.

'Hey, yourself, you lazy slob.' Only then did he allow himself to turn towards her. 'I didn't know napping was included on the agenda today.'

'If I remember correctly, the order for the day was lazing about in the sun on the beach, reading books and a bit of swimming.' She flicked out a finger. 'My nap included lying on the beach *and*—' she flicked out a second finger '—lazing in the sun. So I'm following the remit to the letter, thank you very much.'

The rest had brightened her eyes. And when she stretched her arms back over her head, he noted that her shoulders had lost their hard edge. He noted other things—things that would have

Rupert taking a swing at him if he knew—so he did his best to remove those from his mind.

In one fluid motion, she rose. 'I'm going in for a dip.'

That sounded like an excellent plan. He definitely needed to cool off. Her glance flicked to the scar of his splenectomy when he rose too, and it took an effort to not turn away and hide it from her gaze.

And then she untied her sarong and pulled her T-shirt over her head and it was all he could do to think straight at all.

She nodded at the scar. 'Does it still hurt?'

He touched the indentations and shook his head. 'It didn't really hurt much after it was done either.' At her raised eyebrows he winked. 'Wish I could say the same about the broken ribs.'

She huffed out a laugh, and he was grateful when she moved towards the water's edge without asking any further questions about his accident. Its aftershocks continued to reverberate through him, leaving him at a loss. He didn't know how much longer he'd have to put up with it. He didn't know how much longer he *could* put up with it.

The cold dread that had invaded the pit of his stomach in the moments after his fall invaded him again now, and he broke out in an icy sweat. He'd known in that moment—his skis flying one way and the rest of him going another—that he'd hurt himself badly. He'd understood in a way he never had before that he could die; he had realised he might not make it off the mountain alive.

And every instinct he'd had had screamed a protest against that fate. He hadn't wanted to die, not yet. There were things he wanted— *yearned*—to do. If he'd had breath to spare he'd have begged the medical team to save him. But there'd been no breath to spare, and he'd started spiralling in and out of consciousness.

When he'd awoken from surgery…the relief and gratitude…there were no words to describe it. But for the life of him, now that he was all but recovered, he couldn't remember the things he'd so yearned to do—the reasons why staying alive had seemed so urgent.

All of it had left him with an utter lack of enthusiasm for any of the previous high-octane sports that had once sung to his soul. Had he lost his nerve? He didn't think so. He didn't feel afraid. He just—

A jet of water hit him full in the face and shook him immediately out of his thoughts. 'Lighten up, Finn. I'd have not mentioned the scar if I'd known it'd make you so grim. Don't worry. I'm sure the girls will still fall at your feet with the same old regularity. The odd scar will probably add to your mystique.'

She thought he was brooding for reasons of... *vanity*?

She laughed outright at whatever she saw in his face. 'You're going to pay for that,' he promised, scooping water up in his hands.

They were both soaked at the end of their water fight. Audra simply laughed and called him a bully when he picked her up and threw her into the sea.

He let go of her quick smart, though, because she was an armful of delicious woman...and he couldn't go there. Not with her. 'Race you out to the buoy.'

'Not a chance.' She caressed the surface of the water with an unconscious sensuality that had his gut clenching. 'I'm feeling too Zen after that meditation. And, if you'll kindly remember, there's no racing on today's agenda, thank you very much.'

'Wait until tomorrow.'

She stuck her nose in the air. 'Please don't disturb me while I'm living in the moment.'

With a laugh, he turned and swam out to the buoy. He didn't rush, but simply relished the way his body slid through the water, relished how good it felt to be rid of the cast. He did five laps there and back before his left arm started up a dull ache…and before he could resist finding out what Audra was up to.

He glanced across at where she floated on her back, her face lifted to the sky. He couldn't tell from here whether she had her eyes open or closed. She looked relaxed—now. And while *now* she might also be all grown up, during their water fight she'd laughed and squealed as she had when a girl.

He had a feeling, though, that when her short holiday was over all that tension would descend on her again, pulling her tight. Because…?

Because she wasn't doing the things that gave her joy, wasn't living the life that she should be living. And he had a growing conviction that this wasn't a new development, but an old one he'd never picked up on before. He had no idea how to broach the topic either. She could be undeniably prickly, and she valued her privacy. *Just like you do.* She'd tell him to take a flying leap and mind his own business. And that'd be that.

Walk away. He didn't do encouraging confidences. He didn't do complicated. And it didn't matter which way he looked at it—Audra had always been complicated. Fun and laughter, those were his forte.

He glided through the water towards her until he was just a couple of feet away. 'Boo.'

He didn't shout the word, just said it in a normal tone, but she started so violently he immediately felt sick to his gut. She spun around, the colour leaching from her face, and he wanted to kick himself—hard. 'Damn, Audra, I didn't mean to scare the living daylights out of you.'

She never used to startle this easily. What the hell had happened to change that?

None of the scenarios that played in his mind gave him the slightest bit of comfort.

'Glad I didn't grab you round the waist to tug you under, which had been my first thought.' He said it to try to lighten the moment. When they were kids they all used to dunk each other mercilessly.

If possible she went even paler. And then she ducked under the water, resurfacing a moment later to slick her hair back from her face. 'Note to self,' she said with remarkable self-possession, though he noted the way her hands shook. 'Don't practise meditation in the sea when Finn is around.'

He wanted to apologise again, but it'd be making too big a deal out of it and he instinctively knew that would make her defensive.

'I might head in.' She started a lazy breast-stroke back towards the shore. 'How many laps did you do?'

'Just a couple.' Had she been watching him?

'How does the arm feel?'

He bit back a snap response. *It's fine. And can we just forget about my accident already?* She didn't deserve that. She had to know he didn't like talking about his injuries, but if this was the punishment she'd chosen for his ill-timed *Boo* then he'd take it like a man. 'Dishearteningly weak.'

Her gaze softened. 'You'll get your fitness back, Finn. Just don't push it too hard in these early days.'

He'd had every intention of getting to Kyanós and then swimming and running every day without mercy until he'd proven to himself that he was as fit as he'd been prior to his accident. And yet he found himself more than content at the moment to keep pace beside her. He rolled his shoulders. He'd only been here a couple of days. That old fire would return to his belly soon enough.

He pounced on the cooler bag as soon as he'd towelled off. 'I'm famished.'

He tossed her a peach, which she juggled, nearly dropped and finally caught. He grinned and bit into a second peach. The fragrant flesh and sweet juice hitting the back of his throat tasted better than anything he'd eaten in the last eight weeks. He groaned his pleasure, closing his eyes to savour it all the more. When he opened his eyes again, he found her staring at him as if she'd never seen him before.

Hell, no! Don't look at me like that, Audra.

Like a woman who looked at a man and considered his...um...finer points. It made his skin go hot and tight. It made him want to reach out, slide a hand behind the back of her head and pull her close and—

He glanced out to sea, his pulse racing. He wanted to put colour back into her cheeks, but not like that. The two of them were like oil and water. If he did something stupid now, it'd impact on his relationship with her entire family, and the Russels and his uncle Ned were the only family he had.

He dragged in a gulp of air. Given his current

state of mind, he had to be hyper-vigilant that he didn't mess all this up. He had a history of bringing trouble to the doors of those he cared about—Rupert all those years ago, and now Joachim. Rupert was right—Audra had been through enough. He had no intention of bringing more trouble down on her head.

He forced his stance to remain relaxed. 'Wanna go for a run?'

'A run?' She snapped away and then stared at him as if he'd lost his mind. Which was better. Much *much* better. 'Do you not know me at all?'

He shrugged. 'It was worth a shot.'

'No running, no rushing, no racing.' She ticked the items off her fingers. 'Those are the rules for today. I'm going to explore the rock pools.'

He followed because he couldn't help it. Because a question burned through him and he knew he'd explode if he didn't ask it.

They explored in silence for ten or fifteen minutes. 'Audra?' He worked hard to keep his voice casual.

'Hmm?'

'What the hell did that bastard Farquhar do to you?'

She froze, and then very slowly turned. 'Wow, excellent tactic, Sullivan. Don't get your way over going for a run so hit a girl with an awkward question instead.'

A question he noted she hadn't answered. He rolled with it. 'I work with what I've got.'

Her hands went to her waist. She wore her T-shirt again but not her sarong, and her legs… Her legs went on and on…and on. Where had she been hiding them? 'Who's this woman in Nice you're trying to avoid?'

Oho! So Rupert had told her about that. 'You answer my question, and I'll answer any question you want.'

Her brows rose. *'Any* question?'

'Any time you want to ask it.'

CHAPTER FIVE

ANY TIME SHE wanted to ask it?

That meant… Audra's mind raced. That meant if Finn were running hell for leather, doing laps as if training for a triathlon, risking his neck as if there were no tomorrow, then…then she could ask a question and he'd have to stop and answer her?

Oh, she'd try other stalling tactics first. She wasn't wasting a perfectly good question if she could get him to slow down in other ways, but…

She tried to stop her internal glee from showing. 'You have yourself a deal.'

Finn readjusted his stance. 'So what's the story with Farquhar? The bit that didn't make the papers.'

She hiked herself up to sit on a large rock, its top worn smooth, but its sides pitted with the effects of wind and sand. It was warm beneath her hands and thighs.

He settled himself beside her. 'Is it hard to talk about?'

She sent him what she hoped was a wry glance. 'It's never fun to own up to being a fool...or to having made such a big mistake.'

'Audra—'

She waved him silent. 'I'm surprised you don't know the story.' She'd have thought Rupert would've filled him in.

'I know what was in the paper but not, I suspect, the whole story.'

Dear Rupert. He'd kept his word.

Oddly, though, she didn't mind Finn knowing the story in its entirety. While they might've been friendly adversaries all these years, he was practically family. He'd have her best interests at heart, just as she did his.

'Right.' She slapped her hands to her thighs and he glanced down at them. His face went oddly tight and he immediately stared out to sea. A pulse started up in her throat and her heart danced an irregular pattern in her chest.

Stop it. Don't think of Finn in that way.

But...he's hot.

And he thinks you're hot.

Nonsense! He's just... He just found it hard to not flirt with every woman in his orbit.

She forced herself to bring Thomas's face to mind and the pulse-jerking and heart-hammering came to a screeching halt. 'So the part that everyone knows—' the part that had made the papers '—is that Thomas Farquhar and I had been dating for over seven months.'

Wary brown eyes met hers and he gave a nod. 'What made you fall for him?'

She shrugged. 'He seemed so...*nice*. He went out of his way to spend time with me, and do nice things for me. It was just...nice,' she finished lamely. He'd been so earnest about all the things she was earnest about. He'd made her feel as if she were doing exactly what she ought to be doing with her life. She'd fallen for all of that intoxicating attention and validation hook, line and sinker.

'But it's clear now that he was only dating me to steal company secrets.' A fact the entire world now knew thanks to the tabloids. She shrivelled up a little more inside every time she thought about it.

The Russel Corporation, established by her Swiss grandfather sixty years ago, had originally been founded on a watchmaking dynasty but was now made up of a variety of concerns, including a large charitable arm. Her father was the CEO, though Rupert had been groomed to take over and, to all intents and purposes, was running the day-to-day operations of the corporation.

Her siblings were champions of social justice, each in their own way, just as her parents and grandparents had been in their younger days. Their humanitarian activities were administered by the Russel Corporation, and, as one of the corporation's chief operation managers, Audra had the role of overseeing a variety of projects— from hiring the expertise needed on different jobs and organising the delivery of necessary equipment and goods, to wrangling with various licences and permissions that needed to be secured, and filling in endless government grant forms. And in her spare time she fundraised. It was hectic, high-powered and high-stakes.

For the last five years her sister, Cora, a scientist, had been working on developing a new breakthrough vaccine for the Ebola virus. While such a vaccine would help untold sufferers of the illness, it also had the potential to make pharmaceutical companies vast sums of money.

She tried to slow the churning of her stomach. 'Thomas was after Cora's formulae and research. We know now that he was working for a rival pharmaceutical company. We suspect he deliberately targeted me, and that our meeting at a fundraising dinner wasn't accidental.'

From the corner of her eye she saw Finn nod. She couldn't look at him. Instead she twisted her hands together in her lap and watched the progress of a small crab as it moved from one rock pool to another. 'He obviously worked out my computer password. There were times when we were in bed, when I thought he was asleep, and I'd grab my laptop to log in quickly just to check on something.'

She watched in fascination as his hand clenched and then unclenched. 'You'd have had to have more than one password to get anywhere near Cora's data.'

'Oh, I have multiple passwords. I have one for my laptop, different ones for my desktop computers at home and work. There's the password for my Russel Corporation account. And each of the projects has its own password.' There'd been industrial espionage attempts before. She'd been briefed on internet and computer security. 'But it appears he'd had covert cameras placed around my apartment.'

'How...?'

How did he get access? 'I gave him a key.' She kept her voice flat and unemotional. She'd given an industrial spy unhampered access to her flat—what an idiot! 'I can tell you now, though, that all those romantic dinners he made for us—' his pretext for needing a key '—have taken on an entirely different complexion.' It'd seemed mean-spirited not to give him a key at the time, especially as he'd given her one to his flat.

He swore. 'Did he have cameras in the bedroom?'

'No.' He'd not sunk that low. But it didn't leave her feeling any less violated. 'But...but he must've seen me do some stupid, ugly, unfeminine things on those cameras. And I know it's nothing on the grand scale, but...it *irks* me!'

'What kind of things?'

She slashed a hand through the air. 'Oh, I don't know. Like picking my teeth or hiking my knickers out from uncomfortable places, or... Have you ever seen a woman put on a pair of brandnew sixty-denier opaque tights?'

He shook his head.

'Well, it's not sexy. It looks ludicrous and contortionist and it probably looks hilarious and... And I feel like enough of a laughing stock without him having footage of that too.'

A strong arm came about her shoulder and pulled her in close. Just for a moment she let herself sink against him to soak up the warmth and the comfort. 'He played me to perfection,' she whispered. 'I didn't suspect a damn thing. I thought—' She faltered. 'I thought he liked me.'

His arm tightened about her. 'He was a damn fool. The man has to be a certifiable idiot to choose money over you, sweetheart.'

He pressed his lips to her hair and she felt an unaccountable urge to cry.

She didn't want to cry!

'Stop it.' She pushed him away and leapt down from the rock. 'Don't be nice to me. My stupidity nearly cost Cora all of the hard work she's put in for the last five years.'

'But it didn't.'

No, it hadn't. And it was hard to work up an outraged stomp in flip-flops, and with the Aegean spread before her in twinkling blue perfection and the sun shining down as if the world was full of good things. The files Thomas had stolen were old, and, while to an outsider the formulae and hypotheses looked impressive, the work was neither new nor ground-breaking. Audra didn't have access to the information Thomas had been so anxious to get his hands on for the simple fact that she didn't need it. The results of

Cora's research had nothing to do with Audra's role at work.

But Thomas didn't know that yet. And there was a court case pending. 'So...' She squinted into the sun at him. 'Rupert told you that much, huh?'

'I didn't know about the hidden cameras, but as for the rest...' He nodded.

'You know that's all classified, right?'

He nodded again. 'What hasn't Rupert told me?' He dragged in a breath, his hands clenching. 'Did Farquhar break your heart?'

She huffed out a laugh. 'Which of those questions do you want me to answer first?' When he didn't answer, she moved back to lean against the rock. 'I'll answer the second first because that'll move us on nicely to the first.' She winced at the bitterness that laced her *nicely*. 'No, he didn't break my heart. In fact I was starting to feel smothered by him so I...uh...'

'You...?'

'I told him I wanted to break up.'

He stared at her for a long moment. The muscles in his jaw tensed. 'What did he do?'

She swallowed. 'He pushed me into the hall closet and locked me in.'

He swore and the ferocity of his curse made

her blink. He landed beside her, his expression black.

'I... I think he panicked when I demanded my key back. So he locked me in, stole my computer and high-tailed it out of there.'

'How long were you in there?'

'All night.' And it'd been the longest night of her life.

'How...?'

He clenched his fists so hard he started to shake. In a weird way his outrage helped.

'How did you get out?'

'He made the mistake of using my access code to get into the office early the next morning. Very early when he didn't think anyone else would be around. But Rupert, who had jet lag, had decided to put in a few hours. He saw the light on in my office, and came to drag me off to breakfast.' She shrugged. 'He found Thomas rifling through my filing cabinets instead. The first thing he did was to call Security. The second was to call my home phone and then my mobile. Neither of which I could answer. He has a key to my flat, so...'

'So he raced over and let you out.'

'Yep.'

She'd never been happier to see her older

brother in her life. Her lips twisted. 'It was only then, though, that I learned of the extent of Thomas's double-dealing. And all I wanted to do was crawl back in the closet and hide from the world.'

'Sweetheart—'

She waved him quiet again. 'I know all the things you're going to say, Finn, but don't. Rupert's already said them. *None of this is my fault. Anyone can be taken in by a conman... Blah-blah-blah.*'

She moved to the edge of the rock shelf and stared out at the sea, but its beauty couldn't soothe her. She'd been taken in by a man whose interest and undivided attention had turned her head—a man who'd seemed not only interested but invested in hearing about her hopes and dreams…and supporting her in those dreams. She hadn't felt the focus of somebody's world like that since her mother had died.

She folded her arms, gripped her elbows tight. But it'd all been a lie, and in her hunger for that attention she'd let her guard down. It'd had the potential to cause untold damage to Cora's career, not to mention the Russel Corporation's reputation. She'd been such an idiot!

And to add insult to injury she'd spent the best

part of six weeks trying to talk herself out of breaking up with him because he'd seemed so darn perfect.

Idiot! Idiot! Idiot!

'So now you feel like a gullible fool who's let the family down, and you look at every new person you meet through the tainted lens of suspicion—wondering if they can be trusted or if they're just out for whatever they can get.'

Exactly. She wanted to dive into the sea and power through the water until she was too tired to think about any of this any more. It was a decent swim from here back to the beach, but one that was within her powers. Only…if she did that Finn would follow and five laps out to the buoy and back was enough for him for one day.

She swung around to meet his gaze. 'That sounds like the voice of experience.'

He shrugged and moved to stand beside her, his lips tightening as he viewed the horizon. 'It's how I'd feel in your shoes.'

'Except you'd never be so stupid.' She turned and started to pick her way back along the rock pools towards the beach.

'I've done stupider things with far less cause.'

He had? She turned to find him staring at her with eyes as turbulent as the Aegean in a storm.

She didn't press him, but filed the information away. She might ask him about that some day.

'And even Rupert isn't mistake free. Getting his heart broken by Brooke Manning didn't show a great deal of foresight.'

'He was young,' she immediately defended. 'And we all thought she was as into him as he was into her.'

He raised an eyebrow, and she lifted her hands. 'Okay, okay. I know. It's just... Rupert's mistake didn't hurt anyone but himself. My mistake had the potential to ruin Cora's life's work to date and impact on the entire Russel Corporation, and—'

Warm hands descended to her shoulders. 'But it didn't. Stop focussing on what could have happened and deal with what actually did happen. And the positives that can be found there.'

'Positives?' she spluttered.

'Sure.'

'Oh, I can't wait to hear this. C'mon, wise guy, name me one positive.'

He rubbed his chin. 'Well, for starters, you'd worked out Farquhar was a jerk and had kicked his sorry butt to the kerb.'

Not exactly true. She'd just been feeling suffocated, and hadn't been able to hide from that fact any more.

'And don't forget that's been caught on camera too.'

She stared up at him. And a slow smile built through her. 'Oh, my God.'

He cocked an eyebrow.

'He argued about us breaking up. He wanted me to reconsider and give him another chance.'

'Not an unusual reaction.'

'I told him we could still see each other as friends.'

Finn clutched his chest as if he'd been shot through the heart. 'Ouch!'

'And then he ranted and paced for a bit, and when he had his back to me a few times I, uh, rolled my eyes and...'

'And?'

'Checked my watch because there was a programme on television I was hoping to catch.'

He barked out a laugh.

'And this is embarrassing, for him, so I shouldn't tell it.'

'Yes, you should. You *really* should.'

'Well, he cried. Obviously they were crocodile tears, but I wasn't to know that at the time. I went to fetch the box of tissues, and while my back was to him I pulled this horrible kind of "God help me" face at the wall.'

She gave him a demonstration and he bent at the waist and roared. 'Crocodile tears or not, that's going to leave his ego in shreds. I'm sorry, sweetheart, but getting caught picking your nose suddenly doesn't seem like such a bad thing.'

'I do *not* pick my nose.' She stuck that particular appendage in the air. But Finn was right. She found she didn't care quite so much if Thomas had seen her pigging out on chocolate or dancing to pop music in her knickers. Now whenever she thought about any of those things she'd recall her hilarious grimace—probably straight at some hidden camera—and would feel partially vindicated.

She swung to Finn. 'Thank you.'

'You're welcome.'

They reached the beach and shook sand off their towels, started the five-minute climb back up the hill to the villa. 'Audra?'

'Hmm?'

'I'm sorry I scared you when I arrived the other night. I'm sorry I scared you with my *boo* out there.' He waved towards the water.

She shrugged. 'You didn't mean to.'

'No, I didn't mean to.'

And his voice told her he'd be careful it wouldn't happen again. Rather than being irked at being treated with kid gloves, she felt strangely cared for.

'I guess I owe you an answer now to your question about the woman in Nice who I'm avoiding.'

'No, thank you very much. I mean, you *do* owe me an answer to a question—that was the deal. But I'm not wasting it getting the skinny on some love affair gone wrong.'

He didn't say anything for a long moment. 'What's your question, then?'

'I don't know yet. When I do know I'll ask it.' And then he'd have to stop whatever he was doing and take a timeout to answer it. *Perfect.*

Finn studied Audra across the breakfast table the next morning. Actually, their breakfast table had become the picnic table that sat on the stone terrace outside, where they could drink in the glorious view. She'd turned down the bacon and eggs, choosing cereal instead. He made a mental note to buy croissants the next time they were in the village.

'What are you staring at, Finn?'

He wanted to make sure she was eating enough. But he knew exactly how well that'd go down if he admitted as much. 'I'm just trying to decide if that puny body of yours is up to today's challenge, Russel.'

A spark lit the ice-blue depths of her eyes, but then she shook her head as if realising he was trying to goad her into some kind of reaction. 'This puny body is up for a whole lot more lazing on a beach and a little bobbing about in the sea.'

'Nice try, sweetheart.'

She rolled her eyes. 'What horrors do you have planned?'

'You'll see.' He was determined that by the time she left the island she'd feel fitter, healthier and more empowered than she had when she'd arrived.

She harrumphed and slouched over her muesli, but her gaze wandered out towards the light gleaming on the water and it made her lips lift and her eyes dance. Being here—taking a break—had already been good for her.

But he wanted her to have fun too. A workout this morning followed by play this afternoon. That seemed like a decent balance.

'You want us to what?'

An hour later Audra stared at him with such undisguised horror it was all he could do not to laugh. If he laughed, though, it'd rile her and he didn't want her riled. Unless it was the only way to win her cooperation.

'I want us to jog the length of the beach.'

Her mouth opened and closed. 'But…why? How can this be fun?'

'Exercise improves my mood.' It always had. As a teenager it'd also been a way to exorcise his demons. Now it just helped to keep him fit and strong. He *liked* feeling fit and strong.

He waited for her to make some crack about being in favour of anything that improved his mood. Instead she planted her hands on her hips and stared at him. She wore a silky caftan thing over her swimsuit and the action made it ride higher on her thighs. He tried not to notice.

'Your mood has been fine since you've been here. Apart from your foul temper when you first arrived.'

'You mean when the police had me in hand-cuffs?'

She nodded.

'I'd like to see how silver-tongued you'd be in that situation!'

She smirked and he realised she'd got the rise out of him that she'd wanted, and he silently cursed himself. He fell for it every single time.

'But apart from that blip your mood has been fine.'

She was right. It had been. Which was strange because he'd been an absolute bear in Nice. He'd been a bear since the accident.

He shook that thought off. 'And we want to keep it that way.'

'But—' she gestured '—that has to be nearly a mile.'

'Yep.' He stared at her downturned mouth, imagined *again* that mongrel Farquhar shoving her in a cupboard, and wanted to smash something. He didn't want to bully her. If she really hated the idea... 'Is there any medical reason why you shouldn't run?'

She eyed him over the top of her sunglasses. 'No. You?'

'None. Running ten miles is out of the question, but one mile at a gentle pace will be fine.' He'd checked with his doctors.

'I haven't run since I was a kid. I work in an office...sit behind a desk all day. I'm not sure I can run that far.'

He realised then that her resistance came from a sense of inadequacy.

'I mean, even banged up you're probably super fit and—'

'We'll take it slow. And if you can't jog all the way, we'll walk the last part of it.'

'And you won't get grumpy at me for holding you back?'

'I promise.'

'No snark?'

He snorted. 'I'm not promising that.'

That spark flashed in her eyes again. 'Slow, you said?'

'Slow,' he promised.

She hauled in a breath. 'Well, here goes nothing...'

He started them slowly as promised. It felt good to be running again, even if it was at half his usual pace. Audra started a bit awkwardly, a trifle stiffly, as if the action were unfamiliar, but within two minutes she'd found a steady rhythm and he couldn't help but admire her poise and balance.

That damn ponytail, though, threatened his balance every time he glanced her way, bobbing with a cheeky nonchalance that made things inside him clench up...made him lose his tempo and stray from his course and have to check himself and readjust his line.

At the five-minute mark she was covered in a fine sheen of perspiration, and he suddenly flashed to a forbidden image of what she might look like during an athletic session of lovemaking. He stumbled and broke out into a cold sweat.

Audra seemed to lose her rhythm then too. Her elbows came in tight at her sides…she started to grimace…

And then her hands lifted to her breasts and he nearly fell over. She pulled to a halt and he did too. He glanced at her hands. She reefed them back to her sides and shot him a dark glare. 'Look, you didn't warn me that this is what we'd be doing before we hit the beach.'

Because he hadn't wanted her sniping at him the entire time they descended the hill.

'But they created exercise gear for a reason, you know? If I'm going to jog I need to wear a sports bra.'

He stared at her, not comprehending.

'It hurts to run without one,' she said through gritted teeth.

He blinked. *Hell.* He hadn't thought about that. She wasn't exactly big-breasted, but she was curvy where it mattered and…

'And while we're at it,' she ground out, 'I'd prefer to wear jogging shoes than run barefoot. This is darn hard on the ankles.' Her hands went to her hips. 'For heaven's sake, Finn, you have to give a girl some warning so she can prepare the appropriate outfit.'

He felt like an idiot. 'Well, let's just walk the rest of the way.'

It was hell walking beside her. Every breath he took was scented with peaches and coconut. And from the corner of his eye he couldn't help but track the perky progress of her ponytail. In his mind's eye all he could see was the way she'd cupped her breasts, to help take their weight while running, and things inside him twisted and grew hot.

When they reached the tall cliff at the beach's far end, Audra slapped a hand to it in a 'we made it' gesture. 'My mood doesn't feel improved.'

She sounded peeved, which made him want to laugh. But those lips…that ponytail… He needed a timeout, a little distance. *Now.*

She straightened and gave him the once-over. 'You're not even sweating the tiniest little bit!'

Not where she could see, at least. For which he gave thanks. But he needed to get waist-deep in water soon before she saw the effect she was having on him.

He gestured back the way they'd come. 'We're

going to swim back.' Cold water suddenly seemed like an excellent plan.

Her face fell. 'Why didn't you say so before? I don't want to get my caftan wet. I could've left it behind.'

He was glad she hadn't. The less on show where she was concerned, the better.

'It'll take no time at all to dry off at the other end.'

'It's not designed to be swum in. It'll fall off my shoulder and probably get tangled in my legs.'

He clenched his jaw tight. *Not* an image he needed in his mind.

'I won't be able to swim properly.'

He couldn't utter a damn word.

Her chin shot up. 'You think I'm trying to wriggle my way out, don't you? You think I'm just making up excuses.'

It was probably wiser to let her misinterpret his silence than tell her the truth.

'Well, fine, I'll show you!'

She pulled the caftan over her head and tossed it to him. He did his best not to notice the flare of her hips, the long length of her legs, or the gentle swell of her breasts.

'I'll swim while you keep my caftan dry, cabana boy.'

Her, in the water way over there? Him, on the beach way over here? Worked for him.

'But when we reach the other end it's nothing but lazing on the beach and reading books till lunchtime.'

'Deal.' He was looking forward to another session with his book.

He kept pace with her on the shore, just in case she got a cramp or into some kind of trouble. She alternated freestyle with breaststroke and backstroke. And the slow easy pace suited him. It helped him find his equilibrium again. It gave him the time to remind himself in detail of all the ways he owed Rupert.

He nodded. He owed Rupert big-time—and that meant Audra was off limits and out of bounds. It might be different if Finn were looking to settle down, but settling down and Finn were barely on terms of acquaintance. And while he might feel as if he were at a crossroads in his life, that didn't mean anything. The after-effects of his accident would disappear soon enough. When they did, life would return to normal. He'd be looking for his next adrenaline rush and…and he'd be content again.

* * *

'Jetskiing?'

Audra stared at him with... Well, it wasn't horror at least. Consternation maybe? 'We had a laze on the beach, read our books, had a slow leisurely lunch...and now it's time for some fun.'

She rolled her bottom lip between her teeth. 'But aren't jetskis like motorbikes? And motorbikes are dangerous.'

He shook his head. 'Unlike a motorbike, it doesn't hurt if you fall off a jetski.' At least, not at the speeds they'd be going. 'They're only dangerous if we don't use them right...if we're stupid.'

'But we're going to be smart and use them right?'

He nodded. 'We're even going to have a lesson first.' He could teach her all she needed to know, but he'd come to the conclusion it might be *wiser* to not be so hands-on where Audra was concerned.

She stared at the jetskiers who were currently buzzing about on the bay. 'A lesson?' She pursed her lips. 'And...and it doesn't look as if it involves an awful lot of strength or stamina,' she said, almost to herself. And then she started and jutted her chin. 'Call me a wimp if you want, but

I have a feeling I'm going to be sore enough to-morrow as it is.'

'If you are, the best remedy will be a run along the beach followed by another swim.'

She tossed her head. 'In your dreams, cabana boy.'

He grinned. It was good to see her old spark return. 'This is for fun, Audra, and no other reason. Just fun.'

He saw something in her mind still and then click. 'I guess I haven't been doing a whole lot of that recently.'

She could say that again.

'Okay, well…where do we sign up?'

There were seven of them who took the lesson, and while Finn expected to chafe during the hour-long session, he didn't. It was too much fun watching Audra and her cheeky ponytail as she concentrated on learning how to manoeuvre her jetski. They had a further hour to putter around the bay afterwards to test out her new-found skills. He didn't go racing off on his own. He didn't want her trying to copy him and coming to grief. They'd practised what to do in case of capsizing, but he didn't want them to have to put it into practice. Besides, her laughter and the way her eyes sparkled were too much fun to miss out on.

'Oh, my God!' She practically danced on the dock when they returned their jetskis. 'That was the best fun ever. I'm definitely doing that again. Soon!'

He tried to stop staring at her, tried to drag his gaze from admiring the shape of her lips, the length of her legs, the bounce of her hair. An evening spent alone with her in Rupert's enormous villa rose in his mind, making him sweat. 'Beer?' Hanging out in a crowd for as long as they could suddenly struck him as a sound strategy.

'Yes, please.'

They strode along the wooden dock and he glanced at her from the corner of his eye. The transformation from two days ago was amazing. She looked full of energy and so...*alive.*

He scrubbed both hands back through his hair. Why *was* she hell-bent on keeping herself on such a tight leash? Why didn't she let her hair down once in a while? Why...?

The questions pounded at him. He pressed both hands to the crown of his head in an effort to tamp them down, to counter the impulse to ask her outright. The thing was, even if he did break his protocol on asking personal questions and getting dragged into complicated emotional dilemmas, there was no guarantee Audra would confide in him. She'd never seen him as that kind of guy.

What if she needs to talk? What if she has no one else to confide in?

He wanted to swear.

He wanted to run.

He also wanted to see her filled with vitality and enthusiasm and joy, as she was now.

They ordered beers from a beachside bar and sat at a table in the shade of a jasmine vine to drink them.

'Today has been a really good day, Finn. Thank you.'

Audra wasn't like the women he dated. If she needed someone to confide in, he could be there for her, couldn't he? He took a long pull on his beer. 'Even the running?'

'Ugh, no, the running was awful.' She sipped her drink. 'I can't see I'm ever going to enjoy that, even with the right gear. Though I didn't mind the swimming. There's bound to be a local gym at home that has a pool.'

She was going to keep up the exercise when she returned home? Excellent.

He leaned back, a plan solidifying in his gut. 'You haven't asked your question yet.'

'I already told you—I don't want to hear about your woman in Nice. If you want to brag or grumble about her go right ahead. But I'm not wasting a perfectly good question on it.'

He wondered if he should just tell her about Trixie, but dismissed the idea. Trixie had no idea where he was. She wouldn't be able to cause any trouble here for him, for Joachim or for Audra. And he wanted to keep the smile, the sense of exhilaration, on Audra's face.

He stretched back, practically daring Audra to ask him a question. 'Isn't there anything personal you want to ask me?'

CHAPTER SIX

DID FINN HAVE any clue how utterly mouth-wateringly gorgeous he looked stretched out like that, as if for her express delectation? Audra knew he didn't mean anything by it. Flirting was as natural to him as breathing. If he thought for a moment she'd taken him seriously, he'd backtrack so fast it'd almost be funny.

Almost.

And she wasn't an idiot. Yet she couldn't get out of her mind the idea of striding around the table and—

No, not striding, *sashaying* around the table to plant herself in his lap, gently because she couldn't forget his injuries, and running her hand across the stubble of his jaw before drawing his lips down to hers.

Her mouth went dry and her heart pounded so hard she felt winded...dizzy. Maybe she was an idiot after all.

It was the romance of this idyllic Greek island combined with the euphoria of having whizzed across the water on a jetski. It'd left her feeling wild and reckless. She folded her hands together in her lap. She didn't do wild and reckless. If she went down that path it'd lead to things she couldn't undo. She'd let her family down enough as it was.

Finn folded himself up to hunch over his beer. 'Scrap that. Don't ask your question. I don't like the look on your face. You went from curiously speculative to prim and disapproving.'

She stiffened. 'Prim?'

'Prim,' he repeated, not budging.

'I am *not* prim.'

'Sweetheart, nobody does prim like you.'

His laugh set her teeth on edge. She forced herself to settle back in her chair and to at least appear relaxed. 'I see what you're doing.'

'What am I doing?'

'Reverse psychology. Tell me not to ask a question in the hope I'll do the exact opposite.'

'Is it working?'

'Why are you so fixated on me asking you my owed question?'

A slow grin hooked up one side of his mouth and looking at it was like staring into the sun. She couldn't look away.

'Is that your question?'

Strive for casual.

'Don't be ridiculous.' If Rupert hadn't put the darn notion in her head—*Don't fall for Finn*—she wouldn't be wondering what it'd be like to kiss him.

She sipped her beer. As long as speculation didn't become anything more. She did what she could to ignore the ache that rose through her; to ignore the way her mouth dried and her stomach lurched.

She wasn't starting something with Finn. Even if he proved willing—which he wouldn't in a million years—there was too much at stake to risk it, and not enough to be won. She was *determined* there wouldn't be any more black marks against her name this year. There wouldn't be any more *ever* if she could help it.

If only she could stop thinking about him… *inappropriately*!

For heaven's sake, she was the one in her family who kept things steady, regulated, trouble-free. If there were choppy waters, she was the one who smoothed them. She didn't go rocking the boat and causing drama. That wasn't who she was. She ground her teeth together. And she wasn't going to change now.

She stared out at the harbour and gulped her

beer. This was what happened when she let her hair down and indulged in a bit of impulsive wildness. It was so hard to get her wayward self back under wraps.

Finn might call her prim, but she preferred the terms self-controlled and disciplined. She needed to get things back on a normal grounding with him again, but when she went to open her mouth, he spoke first. 'I guess it's a throwback to the old game of Truth or Dare. I'm not up for too much daredevilry at the moment, but your question—the truth part of the game—is a different form of dangerousness.'

He stared up at the sky, lips pursed, and just like that he was familiar Finn again—family friend. Their session of jetskiing must've seemed pretty tame to him. He'd kept himself reined in for her sake, had focussed on her enjoyment rather than his own. Which meant that dark thread of restlessness would be pulsing through him now, goading him into taking unnecessary risks. She needed to dispel it if she could, to prevent him from doing something daft and dangerous.

'The truth can be ugly, Finn. Admitting the truth can be unwelcome and...' she settled for the word he'd used '...dangerous.'

Liquid brown eyes locked with hers as he drank his beer. He set his glass down on the table and wiped the back of his hand across his mouth. 'I know.'

'And yet you still want me to ask you a possibly dangerous question?'

'I'm game if you are.'

Was there a particular question he wanted her to ask? He stared at her and waited. She moistened her lips again and asked the question that had been rattling around in her mind ever since Rupert's phone call. 'Why do you avoid long-term romantic commitment?'

He blinked. '*That's* what you want to know?'

She shrugged. 'I'm curious. You've never once brought a date to a Russel family dinner. The rest of us have, multiple times. I want to know how you got to avoid the youthful mistakes the rest of us made. Besides...'

'What?'

'When Rupe was warning me off, he made some comment about you not being long-term material. Now we're going to ignore the fact that Rupert obviously thinks women only want long-term relationships when we all know that's simply not true. He obviously doesn't want to think of his little sister in those terms, bless him. But it made me think there's a story there. Hence, my question.'

He nodded, but he didn't speak.

She glanced at his now empty glass. 'If you want another beer, I'm happy to drive us home.'

He called the waiter over and ordered a lime and soda. She did the same. He speared her with a glare. 'I don't need Dutch courage to tell you the truth.'

'And yet that doesn't hide the fact that you don't want to talk about it.' Whatever *it* was. She shrugged and drained the rest of her beer too. 'That's okay, you can simply fob me off with an "I just haven't met the right girl yet" and be done with it.'

'But that would be lying, and lying is against the rules.'

'Ah, so you have met the right girl?' Was it Trixie who'd texted him?

He wagged a finger at her, and just for a moment his eyes danced, shifting the darkness her question had triggered. 'That's an altogether different question. If you'd rather I answer that one…?'

It made her laugh. 'I'll stick with my original question, thank you very much.'

The waiter brought their drinks and Finn took

the straw from his glass and set it on the table. His eyes turned sombre again. 'You know the circumstances surrounding my father's death?'

'He died in a caving accident when you were eight.'

'He liked extreme sports. He was an adrenaline junkie. I seem to have inherited that trait.'

She frowned and sat back.

His eyes narrowed. 'What?'

She took a sip of her drink, wondering at his sharp tone. 'Can one inherit risk-taking the same way they can brown eyes and tawny hair?'

'Intelligence is inherited, isn't it? And a bad temper and... Why?'

He glared and she wished she'd kept her mouth shut. 'Just wondering,' she murmured.

'No, you weren't.'

Fine. She huffed out a breath. 'I always thought your adventuring was a way of keeping your father's memory alive, a way to pay homage to him.'

He blinked.

She tried to gauge the impact her words had on him. 'There isn't any judgement attached to that statement, Finn. I'm not suggesting it's either good or bad.'

He shook himself, but she noted the belligerent thrust to his jaw. 'Does it matter whether my risk-taking is inherited or not?'

'Of course it does. If it's some gene you inherently possess then that means it's always going to be a part of you, a...a natural urge like eating and sleeping. If it's the latter then one day you can simply decide you've paid enough homage. One means you can't change, the other means you can.'

He shoved his chair back, physically moving further away from her, his eyes flashing. She raised her hands. 'But that's not for me to decide. Your call. Like I said, no judgement here. It was just, umm...idle speculation.' She tried not to wince as she said it.

The space between them pulsed with Finn's... outrage? Shock? Disorientation? Audra wasn't sure, but she wanted to get them back on an even keel again. 'What does this have to do with avoiding romantic commitment?'

He gave a low laugh and stretched his legs out in front of him. 'You warned me this could be dangerous.'

It had certainly sent a sick wave of adrenaline coursing through her. 'We don't have to continue with this conversation if you don't want to.'

He skewered her with a glance. 'You don't want to know?'

She ran a finger through the condensation on her glass. He was being honest with her. He deserved the same in return. 'I want to know.'

'Then the rules demand that you get your answer.'

Was he laughing at her?

He grew serious again. 'My father's death was very difficult for my mother.'

Jeremy Sullivan had been an Australian sportsman who for a brief moment had held the world record for the men's four-hundred-metre butterfly. Claudette Dupont, Finn's mother, had been working at the French embassy in Canberra. They'd met, fallen in love and had moved to Europe where Jeremy had pursued a life of adventure and daring. Both of Finn's grandfathers came from old money. They, along with the lucrative sponsorship deals Jeremy received, had funded his and Claudette's lifestyle.

And from the outside it had been an enviable lifestyle—jetting around the world from one extreme sporting event to another—Jeremy taking part in whatever event was on offer while Claudette cheered him from the sidelines. And there'd apparently been everything from cliff diving to ice climbing, bobsledding to waterfall kayaking, and more.

But it had ended in tragedy with the caving accident that had claimed Jeremy's life. Audra dragged in a breath. 'She was too young to be a widow.' And Finn had been too young to be left fatherless.

'She gave up everything to follow him on his adventures—her job, a stable network of friends...a home. She was an only child and there weren't many close relatives apart from her parents.'

Audra wondered how she'd cope in that same situation. 'She had you.'

He shook his head. 'I wasn't enough.'

The pain in his eyes raked through her chest, thickened her throat. 'What happened?' She knew his mother had died, but nobody ever spoke of it.

'She just...faded away. She developed a lot of mystery illnesses—spent a lot of time in hospital. When she was home she spent a lot of time in bed.'

'That's when your uncle Ned came to look after you?' His father's brother was still a big part of Finn's life. He'd relocated to Europe to be with Finn and Claudette.

'He moved in and looked after the both of us. I was eleven when my mother died, and the official verdict was an accidental overdose of painkillers.' He met her gaze. 'Nobody thought she did it deliberately.'

That was something at least. But it was so sad. Such a waste.

'My uncle's verdict was that she'd died of a broken heart.'

Audra's verdict was that Claudette Sullivan had let her son down. Badly. But she kept that to herself. Her heart ached for the little boy she'd left behind and for all the loss he'd suffered.

'Ned blamed my father.'

Wow. 'It must've been hard for Ned,' she offered. 'I don't know what I'd do if I lost one of my siblings. And to then watch as your mother became sicker... He must've felt helpless.'

'He claimed my father should never have married if he wasn't going to settle down to raise a family properly.'

Finn's face had become wooden and she tried not to wince. 'Families aren't one-size-fits-all entities. They don't come in pretty cookie-cutter shapes.'

He remained silent. She moistened her lips. 'What happened after your mother died?'

He straightened in his chair and took a long gulp of lime and soda. 'That's when Ned boarded me at the international school in Geneva. It was full of noisy, rowdy boys and activities specifically designed to keep us busy and out of mischief.'

It was an effort, but she laughed as he'd meant her to. 'I've heard stories about some of the mischief you got up to. I think they need to redesign some of those activities.'

He grinned. 'It was full of life. Ned came to every open day, took me somewhere every weekend we had leave. I didn't feel abandoned.'

Not by Ned, no. But what about his mother? She swallowed. 'And you met Rupert there.'

His grin widened. 'And soon after found myself adopted by the entire Russel clan.'

'For your sins.' She smiled back, but none of it eased the throb in her heart.

'I always found myself drawn to the riskier pastimes the school offered...and that only grew as I got older. There's nothing like the thrill of paragliding down a mountain or surfing thirty-foot waves.'

'Or throwing oneself off a ski jump with gay abandon,' she added wryly, referencing his recent accident.

'Accidents happen.'

But in the pastimes Finn pursued, such accidents could have fatal consequences. Didn't that bother him? 'Did Ned never try and clip your wings or divert your interests elsewhere?' He'd lost a brother. He wouldn't have wanted to lose a nephew as well.

'He's too smart for that. He knew it wouldn't work, not once he realised how determined I was. Before I was of age, when I still needed a guardian's signature, he just made sure I had the very best training available in whatever activity had taken my fancy before he'd sign the permission forms.'

'It must've taken an enormous amount of courage on his behalf.'

'Perhaps. But he'd seen the effect my grandfather's refusals and vetoes had had on my father. He said it resulted in my father taking too many unnecessary chances. In his own way, Ned did his best to keep me safe.'

She nodded.

'The way I live my life, the risks I take, they're not conducive to family life, Audra. When I turned eighteen I promised my uncle to never take an unnecessary risk—to make sure I was always fully trained to perform whatever task I was attempting.'

Thinking about the risks he took made her temples ache.

'I made a promise to myself at the same time.' His eyes burned into hers. 'I swore I'd never become involved in a long-term relationship until I'd given up extreme sports. It's not fair to put any woman through what my father put my mother through.'

It was evident he thought hell had a better chance of freezing over than him ever giving up extreme sports. She eyed him for a moment. 'Have you ever been tempted to break that contract with yourself?'

'I don't break my promises.'

It wasn't an answer. It was also an oblique reminder of the promise he'd made to Rupert. As if that were something she was likely to forget.

'But wouldn't you like a long-term relationship some day? Can't you ever see a time when you'd give up extreme sports?'

His eyes suddenly gleamed. 'Those are altogether separate questions. I believe I've answered your original one.'

Dammit! He had to know that only whetted her appetite for more.

None of your business.

It really wasn't, but then wasn't that the beauty, the temptation, of this game of 'truth or dare' questions—the danger?

Finn wanted to laugh at the quickened curiosity, the look of pique, in Audra's face. He shouldn't play this game. He should leave it all well enough alone, but...

He leaned towards her. 'I'll make a tit-for-tat deal with you.'

Ice-blue eyes shouldn't leave a path of fire on his skin, but beneath her gaze he started to burn. She cocked her head to one side. 'You mean a question-for-question, quid pro quo bargain?'

'Yep.'

She leaned in and searched his face as if trying to decipher his agenda. He did his best to keep his face clear. Finally she eased back and he could breathe again.

'You must be *really* bored.'

He wasn't bored. Her company didn't bore him. It never had. He didn't want to examine that thought too closely, though. He didn't want to admit it out loud either. 'Life has been... quieter of late than usual.'

'And you're finding that a challenge?'

He had in Nice, but now…not really. Which didn't make sense.

Can you inherit a risk-taking gene? He shied away from that question, from the deeper implications that lay beneath its surface. So what if some of his former pursuits had lost their glitter? That didn't mean anything.

He set his jaw. 'Let's call it a new experience.'

Her lips pressed together into a prim line he wanted to mess up. He'd like to kiss those lips until they were plump and swollen and— *Hell!*

'Are you up for my question challenge?' He made his voice deliberately mocking in a way he knew would gall her.

'I don't know. I'll think about it.'

He kinked an eyebrow, deliberately trying to inflame her competitive spirit. 'What are you afraid of?'

She pushed her sunglasses further up her nose and readjusted her sunhat. 'Funny, isn't it, how every question now seems to take on a double edge?'

He didn't pursue it. In all honesty letting sleeping dogs lie would probably be for the best.

Really?

He thrust out his jaw. And if not, then there was more than one way to find out what was troubling her. He just needed to turn his mind to it. Find another way.

Finn laughed when Audra pulled the two trays of croissants from the oven. Those tiny hard-looking lumps were supposed to be croissants? Her face, comical in its indignation, made him laugh harder.

'How can you laugh about this? We spent hours on these and…and *this* is our reward?'

'French pastry has a reputation for being no-toriously difficult, hasn't it?' He poked a finger at the nearest hard lump and it disintegrated to ash beneath his touch. 'Wow, I think we just took French cooking to a new all-time low.'

'But…but you're half French! That should've given us a head start.'

'And you're half Australian but I don't see any particular evidence of that making you handy with either a cricket bat or a barbecue.'

Like Finn's father, Audra's mother had been Australian. Audra merely glowered at him, slammed the cookbook back to the bench top and studied its instructions once again. He hoped she wasn't going to put him through the torture of working so closely beside her in the kitchen again. There'd been too much accidental brushing of arms, too much…heat. Try as he might, he couldn't blame it all on the oven. Even over the smell of flour, yeast and milk, the scent of peaches and coconut had pounded at him, making him hungry.

But not for food.

He opened a cupboard and took out a plate, unwrapped the bakery bag he'd stowed in the pantry earlier and placed half a dozen croissants onto it. He slid the plate towards Audra.

She took a croissant without looking, bit into it and then pointed at the cookbook. 'Here's where we went wrong. We—'

She broke off to stare at the croissant in her hand, and then at the plate. 'If you dare tell me here are some croissants you prepared earlier, I'll—'

'Here are some croissants I *bought* at the village bakery earlier.'

'When earlier?'

'Dawn. Before you were up.'

The croissant hurtled back to the plate and her hands slammed to her hips. He backed up a step. 'I wasn't casting aspersions on your croissant-making abilities. But I wanted a back-up plan because…because I wanted to eat croissants.' Because she'd seemed so set on them.

Her glare didn't abate. 'What else have you been doing at the crack of dawn each morning?'

He shook his head, at a loss. 'Nothing, why?'

'Have you been running into the village and back every morning?'

He frowned. 'I took the car.' Anyway, he wasn't up to running that distance yet. And he hadn't felt like walking. Every day he felt a little stronger, but… It hadn't occurred to him to run into the village. Or to run anywhere for that matter. Except with her on the beach, when it was his turn to choose their daily activities. Only then he didn't make her jog anyway. They usually walked the length of the beach and then swam back.

'Or…or throwing yourself off cliffs or…or kite surfing or—'

He crowded in close then, his own temper rising, and it made her eyes widen…and darken. 'That wouldn't be in the spirit of the deal we made, would it?'

She visibly swallowed. 'Absolutely not.'

'And I'm a man of my word.'

Her gaze momentarily lowered to his lips before lifting again. 'You're also a self-professed adrenaline junkie.'

Except the adrenaline flooding his body at the

moment had nothing to do with extreme sports. It had to do with the perfect shape of Audra's mouth and the burning need to know what she'd taste like. Would she taste of peaches and coconut? Coffee and croissant? Salty or sweet? His skin tightened, stretching itself across his frame in torturous tautness.

Her breathing grew shallow and a light flared to life in her eyes and he knew she'd recognised his hunger, his need, but she didn't move away, didn't retreat. Instead her gaze roved across his face and lingered for a beat too long on his mouth, and her lips parted with an answering hunger.

'A man of his word?' she murmured, swaying towards him.

Her words penetrated the fog surrounding his brain. *What are you doing? You can't kiss her!*

He snapped away, his breathing harsh. Silence echoed off the walls for three heart-rending beats and then he heard her fussing around behind him...dumping the failed croissants in the bin, rinsing the oven trays. 'Thank you for buying backup croissants, Finn.'

He closed his eyes and counted to three, before turning around. He found her surveying him, her tone nonchalant and untroubled—as if she hadn't been about to reach up on her tiptoes and kiss him. He'd seen the temptation in her eyes, but somehow she'd bundled up her needs and desires and hidden them behind a prim wall of control and restraint. It had his back molars grinding together.

He didn't know how he knew, but this was all related—her tight rein on her desires and needs, her refusal to let her hair down and have fun, the dogged determination to repress it all because…?

He had no idea! He had no answer for why she didn't simply reach out and take what she wanted from life.

She bit into her croissant and it was all he could do then not to groan.

'I have a "truth or dare" question for you, Finn.'

He tried to match her coolness and composure. 'So you've decided to take me up on the quid pro quo bargain?'

She nodded and stuck out a hip. If he'd been wearing a tie he'd have had to loosen it. 'If you're still game,' she purred.

In normal circumstances her snark would've had him fighting a grin. But nothing about today and this kitchen and Audra felt the least bit normal. Or the least bit familiar. 'Ask your question.'

She eyed him for a moment, her eyes stormy. 'Don't you want something more out of life?'

'More?' He felt his eyes narrow. 'Like what?'

'I mean, you flit from adventure to adventure, but...' That beautiful brow of hers creased. 'Don't you want something more worthwhile, more...*lasting*?'

His lips twisted. A man showed no interest in settling down—

'I'm not talking about marriage and babies!' she snapped as if reading his mind. 'I'm talking about doing something good with your life, making a mark, leaving a legacy.'

Her innate and too familiar disapproval stung him in ways it never had before. Normally he'd have laughed it off, but...

He found himself leaning towards her. He had to fight the urge to loom. He wasn't Thomas-blasted-Farquhar. He didn't go in for physical intimidation. 'Do you seriously think I *just* live off my trust fund while I go trekking through the Amazon and train for the London marathon, and—'

'Look, I know you raise a lot of money for charity, but there doesn't seem to be any rhyme or reason to your methods—no proper organisation. You simply bounce from one thing to the next.'

'And what about my design company?'

Her hands went to her hips. 'You don't seem to spend a lot of time in the office.'

His mouth worked. 'You think I treat my company like a…a toy?'

'Well, don't you? I mean, you never talk about it!'

'You never ask me about it!'

She blinked. 'From where I'm standing—'

'With all the other workaholics,' he shot back.

'It simply looks as if you're skiving off from the day job to have exciting adventures. Obviously that's your prerogative, as you're the boss, but—'

He raised his arms. 'Okay, we're going to play a game.'

She stared at him. Her eyes throbbed, and he knew that some of this anger came from what had almost happened between them—the physical frustration and emotional confusion. He wanted to lean across and pull her into his arms and hug her until they both felt better. But he had a feeling that solution would simply lead to more danger.

Her chin lifted. 'And what about my question?'

'By the end of the game you'll have your answer. I promise.' And in the process he meant to challenge her to explore the dreams she seemed so doggedly determined to bury.

Her eyes narrowed and she folded her arms. 'What does this game involve?'

'Sitting in the garden with a plate of croissants and my computer.'

She raised her eyebrows. 'Sitting?'

'And eating…and talking.'

She unfolded her arms. 'Fine. That I can do.'

What was it his uncle used to say? *There's more than one way to crack an egg.* He might never discover the reasons Audra held herself back, but the one thing he could do was whet her appetite for the options life held, give her the push she perhaps needed to reach for her dreams. After all, temptation and adventure were his forte. He frowned as he went to retrieve his laptop. At least, they had been once. And he'd find his fire for them again soon enough.

And he couldn't forget that once he'd answered her question, he'd have one of his own in the kitty. He might never use it—she was right, these questions could be dangerous—but it'd be there waiting just in case.

CHAPTER SEVEN

AUDRA BLINKED WHEN Finn handed her a large notepad and a set of pencils. She opened her mouth to ask what they were for, but when he sat opposite and opened his laptop she figured she'd find out soon enough.

For the moment she was simply content to stare at him and wonder what that stubble would feel like against her palms and admire the breadth of his shoulders and—

No, no. *No!*

For the moment she was content to…to congratulate herself for keeping Finn quiet for another day. And she'd…*admire the view.* The brilliant blue of the sea contrasted with the soft blue of the sky, making her appreciate all the different hues on display. A yacht with a pink and blue sail had anchored just offshore and she imagined a honeymooning couple rowing into one of the many deserted coves that lay along this side of the island, and enjoying…

Her mind flashed with forbidden images, and she shook herself. *Enjoying a picnic.*

'Audra?'

She glanced up to find Finn staring at her, one eyebrow raised. She envied that. She'd always wanted to do it. She tried it now, and he laughed. 'What are you doing?'

'I love the "one eyebrow raised" thing. It looks great and you do it really well. I've always wanted to do it, but...' She tried again and he convulsed. Laughter was good. She needed to dispel the fraught atmosphere that had developed between them in the kitchen. She needed to forget about kissing him. He'd been looking grim and serious in odd moments these last few days too...sad, after telling her about the promise he'd made to himself when he'd turned eighteen.

She didn't want him sad. In the past she'd often wanted to get the better of him, but she didn't want that now either. She just wanted to see him fit and healthy. Happy. And she wanted to see him the way she used to see him—as Rupert's best friend. If she focussed hard enough, she could get that back, right?

She gave a mock sigh. 'That's not the effect I was aiming for.'

'There's a trick.'

She leaned towards him. 'Really?'

He nodded.

'Will you tell it to me?'

'If you'll tell me what you were thinking about when you were staring out to sea.' He gestured behind him at the view. 'You were a million miles away.'

Heat flushed her cheeks. She wasn't going to tell him about her imaginary honeymoon couple, but… 'It's so beautiful here. *So* beautiful. It does something to me—fills me up…makes me feel more…'

He frowned. 'More what?'

She lifted her hands only to let them drop again. 'I'm not sure how to explain it. It just makes me feel more…myself.'

He sat back as if her words had punched the air from his lungs. 'If that's true then you should move here.'

'Impossible.' Her laugh, even to her own ears, sounded strained.

'Nothing's impossible.'

She couldn't transplant her work here. She didn't even want to try. It'd simply suck the colour and life from this place for her anyway, so she shook her head. 'It's just a timely reminder that I should be taking my holidays more often.'

She had a ridiculous amount of leave accrued. She had a ridiculous amount of money saved too. Maybe even enough for a deposit on a little cottage in the village? And then, maybe, she could own her own bit of paradise—a bit that was just hers.

And maybe having that would help counter the grey monotony her life in Geneva held for her.

Finn stared at her as if he wanted to argue the point further. No more. Some pipe dreams made her chest ache, and not in a good way. 'Fair's fair. Share your eyebrow-raising tip.'

So he walked her through it. 'But you'll need to practise. You can do an internet search if you want to.'

Really? Who'd have thought?

He rubbed his hands together. 'Now we're going to play my game.'

'And the name of the game...?'

'Designing Audra's favourite...'

'Holiday cottage?' she supplied helpfully.

His grin widened and he clapped his hands. 'Designing Audra's favourite shop.'

Her heart started to pound.

'How old were you when you decided shop-keeping sang to your soul?'

She made herself laugh because it was quite

clearly what he intended. 'I don't know. I guess I must've been about six.' And then eleven… fifteen…seventeen. But her owning a shop—it was a crazy idea. It was so *indulgent*.

But this was just a game. Her heart thumped. It wouldn't hurt to play along for an hour or so. Finn obviously wanted to show off some hidden talent he had and who was she to rain on his parade? The lines of strain around his eyes had eased and the grooves bracketing his mouth no longer bit into his flesh so deeply. Each day had him moving more easily and fluidly. Coming here had been good for him. Taking it easy was good for him. She wanted all that goodness to continue in the same vein.

She made herself sit up straighter. 'Right, the name of the game is Designing Audra's Dream Shop.'

He grinned and it sent a breathless kind of energy zinging through her.

'We're going to let our minds go wild. The sky's the limit. Got it?'

'Got it.'

He held her gaze. 'I mean it. The point of the game is to not be held back by practicalities or mundane humdrummery. That comes later. For this specific point in time we're aiming for best of the best, top of the pops, no compromises, just pure unadulterated dream vision.'

She had a feeling she should make some sort of effort to check the enthusiasm suddenly firing through her veins, but Finn's enthusiasm was infectious. And she was in the Greek islands on holiday. She was allowed to play. She nodded once, hard. 'Right.'

'First question...' his fingers were poised over the keyboard of his computer '...and experience tells me that the first answer that pops into your mind is usually the right one.'

'Okay, hit me with Question One.'

'Where is your ideal location for your shop?'

'Here on Kyanós...in the village's main street, overlooking the harbour. There's a place down there that's for sale and...' she hesitated '...it has a nice view.'

His fingers flew over the keyboard. 'What does your ideal shop sell?'

'Beautiful things,' she answered without hesitation.

'Specifics, please.'

So she described in detail the beautiful things she'd love to sell in her dream shop. 'Handicrafts made by local artisans—things like jade pendants and elegant bracelets, beautiful scented candles and colourful scarves.' She pulled in a breath. 'Wooden boxes ornamented with beaten silver, silver boxes ornamented with coloured beads.' She described gorgeous leather hand-bags, scented soaps and journals made from handcrafted paper.

She rested her chin on her hands and let her mind drift into her dream shop—a pastime she'd refused to indulge in for…well, years now. 'There'd be beautiful prints for sale on the walls. There'd be wind chimes and pretty vases…glass-ware.'

She pulled back, suddenly self-conscious, heat bursting across her cheeks. 'Is that…uh… specific enough?'

'It's perfect.'

He kept tap-tapping away, staring at the com-puter screen rather than at her, and the heat slowly faded from her face. He looked utterly engrossed and she wondered if he'd worn the same expression when he'd set off on his ill-fated ski jump.

He glanced at her and she could feel herself colour again at being caught out staring. Luckily, he didn't seem to notice. He just started shooting questions at her again. How big was her shop? Was it square or rectangle? Where did she want to locate the point of sale? What colour scheme would she choose? What shelving arrangements and display options did she have in mind?

Her head started to whirl at the sheer number of questions, but she found she could answer them all without dithering or wavering, even when she didn't have the correct terminology for what she was trying to describe. Finn had a knack for asking her things and then reframing her answers in a way that captured exactly what she meant. She wasn't sure how he did it.

'Okay, you need to give me about fifteen minutes.'

'I'll get us some drinks.' She made up a fruit and cheese platter to supplement their lunch of croissants, added some dried fruits and nuts before taking the tray outside.

Finn rose and took the tray from her. 'Sit. I'll show you what I've done.'

She did as he bid. He turned the computer to face her.

She gasped. She couldn't help it. She pulled the computer towards her. She couldn't help that either. If she could've she'd have stepped right inside his computer because staring out at her from the screen was the interior of the shop she'd dreamed about ever since she was a little girl—

a dream she'd perfected as she'd grown older and her tastes had changed. 'How…?' She could barely push the word past the lump in her throat. 'How did you do this?'

'Design software.'

He went to press a button, but she batted his hand away. 'Don't touch a thing! This is *perfect*.' It was amazing. The interior of her fantasy shop lived and breathed there on the screen like a dream come true and it made everything inside her throb and come alive.

'Not perfect.' He placed a slice of feta on a cracker and passed it across to her. 'It'd take me another couple of days to refine it for true perfection. But it gives a pretty good indication of your vision.'

It did. And she wanted this vision. She wanted it so bad it tasted like raspberries on her tongue. Instead of raspberries she bit into feta, which was pretty delicious too.

'If you push the arrow key there're another two pictures of your shop's interior from different angles.'

She popped the rest of the cracker into her mouth and pressed the arrow key…and marvelled anew at the additional two pictures that appeared—one from the back of the shop, and one from behind the sales counter, both of which afforded a glorious view of a harbour. There was a tub of colourful flowers just outside the door and her eyes filled. She reached out and touched them. 'You remembered.'

'I did.'

She pored over every single detail in the pictures. She could barely look away from the screen, but she had to. This dream could never be hers. She dragged in a breath, gathered her resources to meet Finn's gaze and to pretend that this hadn't been anything more than a game, an interesting exercise, when her gaze caught on the logo in the bottom right corner of the screen. The breath left her lungs in a rush. She knew that logo!

Her gaze speared to his. '*You're* Aspiration Designs?'

'Along with my two partners.'

He nodded a confirmation and she couldn't read the expression in his eyes. 'How did I not know about this?'

He shrugged. 'It's not a secret.'

'But...your company was called Sullivan Brand Consultants.'

'Until I merged with my partners.'

She forced her mind back to the family dinners and the few other times in recent years that she'd seen Finn, and tried to recall a conversation—any conversation—about him expanding his company or going into partnership. There'd been some vague rumblings about some changes, but…she'd not paid a whole lot of attention. She wanted to hide her face in her hands. Had she really been so uninterested…so set in her picture of who Finn was?

She moistened her lips. Aspiration Designs was a boutique design business in high demand. 'You created the foyer designs for the new global business centre in Geneva.'

He lifted a shoulder in a silent shrug.

Those designs had won awards.

She closed the lid of the laptop, sagging in her seat. 'I've had you pegged all wrong. For all these years you haven't been flitting from one daredevil adventure to another. You've been—' she gestured to the computer '—making people's dreams come true.'

'I don't make people's dreams come true. They make their own dreams come true through sheer hard work and dedication. I just show them what their dream can look like.'

In the same way he'd burned the vision of her dream shop onto her brain.

'And another thing—' he handed her another cracker laden with cheese '—Aspirations isn't a one-man band. My partners are in charge of the day-to-day running. Also, I've built an amazing design team and one of my super-powers is delegation. Which means I can go flitting off on any adventure that takes my fancy, almost at a moment's notice.'

She didn't believe that for a moment. She bet he timed his adventures to fit in with his work demands.

'And in hindsight it's probably not all that surprising that you don't know about my company. How often have we seen each other in the last four or five years? Just a handful of times.'

He had a point. 'Christmas...and occasionally when you're in Geneva I'll catch you when you're seeing Rupert.' But that was often for just a quick drink. They were on the periphery of each other's lives, not inside them.

'And when you do see me you always ask me what my latest adventure has been and where I'm off to next.'

Her stomach churned. Never once had she asked him about his work. She hadn't thought he did much. Instead, she'd vicariously lived adventure and excitement through him. But the same disapproval she directed at herself—to keep herself in check—she'd also aimed at him. How unfair was that!

She'd taken a secret delight in his exploits while maintaining a sense of moral superiority by dismissing them as trivial. She swallowed. 'I owe you an apology. I'm really sorry, Finn. I've been a pompous ass.'

He blinked. 'Garbage. You just didn't know.'

She hadn't wanted to know. She'd wanted to dismiss him as an irresponsible lightweight. Her mouth dried. And in thinking of him as a self-indulgent pleasure-seeker it had been easier to battle the attraction she'd always felt simmering beneath the surface of her consciousness for him.

God! That couldn't be true.

Couldn't it?

She didn't know what to do with such an epiphany, so she forced a smile to uncooperative lips. 'You have your adventures *and* you do good and interesting work. Finn…' she spread her hands '…you're living the dream.'

He laughed but it didn't reach his eyes. She recalled what he'd told her—about the promise he'd made to himself when he'd come of age—and a protest rose through her. 'I think you're wrong, Finn—both you and Ned. I think you *can* have a long-term relationship *and* still enjoy the extreme sports you love.' The words blurted out of her with no rhyme or reason. Finn's head snapped back. She winced and gulped and wished she could call them back.

'Talk about a change of topic.' He eased away, eyed her for a moment. 'Wrong how?'

She shouldn't have started this. But now that she had... She forced herself to straighten. 'I just don't think you can define your own circumstances based on what happened to your parents. And I'm far from convinced Ned should blame your father for everything that happened afterwards.' She raised her hands in a conciliatory gesture. 'I know! I know! He has your best interests at heart. And, look, I love your uncle Ned.' He came to their Christmas dinners and had become as much a part of the extended family as Finn had. 'But surely it's up to you and your prospective life partner to decide what kind of marriage will work for you.'

'But my mother—'

Frustration shot through her. 'Not every woman deals with tragedy in the same way your mother did!'

'Whoa!' He stared at her.

Heck!

'Sorry. Gosh, I…' She bit her lip.

What had she been thinking?

'Sorry,' she said again, swallowing. 'That came out harsher than I meant it to—*way* harsher. I just meant, people react to tragedy in different ways. People react to broken hearts in different ways. I'm not trying to trivialise it; I'm not saying it's easy. It's just…not everyone falls into a decline. If you live by those kinds of rules then—'

He leaned towards her and she almost lost her train of thought. 'Um, then…it follows that *you'd* better never marry a woman who's into extreme sports or…or has a dangerous job because if she dies then you wouldn't be able to survive it.'

His jaw dropped.

'And from the look on your face, it's clear you don't think of yourself as that kind of person.'

He didn't.

Finn stared at Audra, not sure why his heart pounded so hard, or why something chained inside him wanted to suddenly break free.

She retied her ponytail, not quite meeting his eyes. 'I mean, not everyone wants to marry and that's fine. Not everyone wants to have kids, and that's fine too. Maybe you're one of those people.'

'But?'

She bit her bottom lip and when she finally released it, it was plump from where she'd worried at it. She shrugged. 'But maybe you're not.'

'You think I want to marry and have kids?'

Blue eyes met his, and they had him clenching up in strange ways. 'I have no idea.' She leaned towards him the tiniest fraction. 'Wouldn't you eventually like to have children?'

'I don't know.' He'd never allowed himself to think about it before. 'You?'

'I'd love to be a mother one day.'

'Would you marry someone obsessed with extreme sports?'

'I wouldn't marry someone obsessed with anything, thank you very much. I don't want my life partner spending all his leisure time away from me—whether it's for rock climbing, stamp collecting or golf. I'd want him to want to spend time with me.'

Any guy lucky enough to catch Audra's eye would be a fool not to spend time with her. *Lots* of time. As much as he could.

'I don't want *all* of his leisure time, though.' She glared as if Finn had accused her of exactly that. 'There are girlfriends to catch up with over coffee and cake...or cocktails. And books to read.'

Speaking of books, he hoped she had reading down on today's agenda. He wouldn't mind getting back to his book. 'But you'd be okay with him doing some rock climbing, hang-gliding or golf?'

'As long as he doesn't expect me to take up the sport too. I mean, me dangling from a thin rope off a sheer cliff or hurtling off a sheer cliff in a glorified paper plane—what could possibly go wrong?'

A bark of laughter shot out of him. 'We're going to assume that this hypothetical life partner of yours would insist on you getting full training before attempting anything dangerous.'

She wrinkled her nose. 'Doesn't change the fact I'm not the slightest bit interested in rock climbing, hang-gliding or golf. I wouldn't want to go out with someone who wanted to change me.'

He sagged back on the wooden bench, air leaving his lungs. 'Which is why you wouldn't change him.' It didn't mean she wouldn't worry when her partner embarked on some risky activity, but she'd accept them for who they were. She'd want them to be happy.

Things inside him clenched up again. So what if laps around a racetrack had started to feel just plain boring—round and round in endless monotonous laps? *Yawn.* And so what if he couldn't remember why he'd thought hurtling off that ski jump had been a good idea. It didn't mean he wanted to change his entire lifestyle. It didn't mean anything. Yet…

He'd never let himself think about the possibility of having children before. He moistened suddenly dry lips. He wasn't sure he should start now either.

And yet he couldn't let the matter drop. 'Do you think about having children a lot?'

Her brow wrinkled. 'Where are you going with this? It's not like I'm obsessed or anything. It's not like it's constantly on my mind. But I am twenty-seven. Ideally, if I were going to start a family, I'd want that to happen in the next ten years. And I wouldn't want to get married and launch immediately into parenthood. I'd want to enjoy married life for a bit first.'

She frowned then. 'What?' he demanded, curious to see inside this world of hers—unsure if it attracted or repelled him.

'I was just thinking about this hypothetical partner you've landed me with. I hope he understands that things change when babies come along.'

Obviously, but…um. 'How?'

She selected a brazil nut before holding the bowl out to him. 'Suddenly you have way less time for yourself. Cocktail nights with the girls become fewer and farther between.'

He took a handful of nuts. 'As do opportunities to throw yourself off a cliff, I suppose?'

'Exactly.'

Except having Finn hadn't slowed his father down. And his mother certainly hadn't insisted on having a stable home base. She'd simply towed Finn and his nanny along with them wherever they went. And when he was old enough, she hired tutors to homeschool him.

And everything inside him rebelled at blaming his parents for that.

'A baby's needs have to be taken into consideration and—'

She broke off when she glanced into his face. 'I'm not criticising your parents, Finn. I'm not saying they did it wrong or anything. I'm describing how *I'd* want to do it. Each couple works out what's best for them.'

'But you'd want to be hands-on. I have a feeling that nannies and boarding schools and in-home tutors aren't your idea of good parenting. You'd want a house in the suburbs, to host Christmas dinner—'

'It doesn't have to be in the burbs. It could be an apartment in the city or a house overlooking a Greek beach. And if I can afford a nanny I'll have one of those too, thank you very much. I'd want to keep working.'

His parents had chosen to not work. At all.

'But when I get home from work, I'd want to have my family around me. That's all.' Their eyes locked. 'It's not how my parents did it…and I'm not saying I hated boarding school, because I didn't. I know how lucky I've been. I'm not saying my way is better than anybody else's. I'm just saying that's the way that'd make *me* happy.'

She'd just described everything he'd wanted when he was a child, and it made the secret places inside him ache. It also brought something into stark relief. She knew what would make her happy in her personal life—she knew the kind of home life and family that she wanted, and it was clear she wasn't going to settle for less. So why was she settling for less in her work life?

The question hovered on his tongue. He had a 'truth or dare' question owing to him, but something held him back, warned him the time wasn't right. Audra was looking more relaxed with each day they spent here. Her appetite had returned, as had the colour in her cheeks. But he recalled the expression in her eyes when he'd first turned his computer around to show her that shop, and things inside him knotted up. It was too new, and too fragile. She needed more time to pore over those pictures…to dream. He wanted her hunger to build until she could deny it no longer.

He loaded two crackers with cheese and handed her one, before lifting the lid of his computer. 'I'll email those designs through to you.'

'Oh, um…thank you. That'll be fun.'

Fun? Those walls had just gone back up in her eyes. That strange restraint pulled back into place around her. He didn't understand it, but he wasn't going to let her file those pictures away in a place where she could forget about them. He'd use Rupert's office later to print hard copies off as well. She might ignore her email, but she'd find the physical copies much harder to ignore.

'What's on the agenda for the rest of the day?'

She sent him a cat-that-got-the-cream grin. 'Nothing. Absolutely nothing.'

Excellent. 'Books on the beach?'

'You're getting the hang of this, Sullivan.' She rose and collected what was left of the food, and started back towards the house. 'Careful,' she shot over her shoulder, 'you might just find yourself enjoying it.'

He was enjoying it. He just wasn't sure what that meant.

He shook himself. It didn't mean anything, other than relief at being out of hospital and not being confined to quarters. He'd be an ingrate—not to mention made of marble—not to enjoy all this glorious Greek sun and scenery.

And whatever else he was, he wasn't made of marble. With Audra proving so intriguing, this enforced slower pace suited him fine for the moment. Once he got to the bottom of her strange restraint his restlessness would return. And then he'd be eager to embark on his next adventure—in need of a shot of pure adrenaline.

His hunger for adventure would return and consume him, and all strange conversations about children would be forgotten. He rose; his hands clenched. This was about Audra, not him.

Audra stared at the ticket Finn had handed her and then at the large barn-like structure in front of them. She stared down at the paper in her hand again. 'You...you enrolled us in an art class?'

If Finn had been waiting for her to jump up

and down in excitement and delight, he'd have been disappointed.

Which meant… Yeah, he was disappointed.

How had he got this wrong? 'When you saw the flyer in the bookshop window you looked…'

'I looked what?'

Her eyes turned wary with that same damn restraint that was there when she talked about her shop. Frustration rattled through him. Why did she do that?

'Looked what?' she demanded.

'Interested,' he shot back.

Wistful, full of yearning…hungry.

'I can't draw.'

'Which is why it says *"Beginners"*—' he pointed '—right here.'

She blew out a breath.

'What's more I think you were interested, but for some reason it intimidated you, so you chickened out.'

Her chin shot up, but her cheeks had reddened. 'I just didn't think it'd be your cup of tea.'

'You didn't think lying on a beach reading a book would float my boat either, but that didn't stop you. And I've submitted with grace. I haven't made a single complaint about your agendas. Unlike you with mine.'

'Oh!' She took a step back. 'You make me sound mean-spirited.'

She *wasn't* mean-spirited. But she *was* the most frustrating woman on earth!

'I'm sorry, Finn. Truly.' She seemed to gird her loins. 'You've chosen this specifically with me in mind. And I'm touched. Especially as I know you'd rather be off paragliding or aqua boarding or something.'

He ran a finger around the collar of his T-shirt. That wasn't one hundred per cent true. It wasn't even ten per cent true. Not that he had any intention of saying so. 'But?' he countered, refusing to let her off the hook. 'You don't want to do it?'

'It's not that.'

He folded his arms. 'Then what is it?'

'Forget it. You just took me by surprise, is all.' She snapped away from him. 'Let's just go in and enjoy the class and—'

He reached out and curled his hand around hers and her words stuttered to a halt. 'Audra?' He raised an eyebrow and waited.

Her chin shot up again. 'You won't understand.'

'Try me.'

A storm raged in her eyes. He watched it in

fascination. 'Do you ever have rebellious impulses, Finn?'

He raised both eyebrows. 'My entire life is one big rebellion, surely?'

'Nonsense! You're living your life exactly as you think your parents would want you to.'

She snatched her hand back and he felt suddenly cast adrift.

'You've not rebelled any more than I have.'

That wasn't true, but... He glanced at the studio behind her. 'Art class is a rebellion?'

'In a way.'

'How?'

She folded her arms and stared up at the sky. He had a feeling she was counting to ten. 'Look, I can see the sense in taking a break, in having a holiday. Lying on a beach and soaking up some Vitamin D, getting some gentle exercise via a little swimming and walking, reading a book— I see the sense in those things. They lead to a rested body and mind.'

'How is an art class different from any of those things?'

'It just is! It feels...self-indulgent. It's doing something for the sake of doing it, rather than because it's good for you or...or...'

'What about fun?'

She stared at him. 'What's *fun* got to do with it?'

He couldn't believe what he was hearing. 'Evidently nothing.' Was she really that afraid of letting her hair down?

'When I start doing one thing just for the sake of it—*for fun*,' she spat, 'I'll start doing others.'

He lifted his arms and let them drop. 'And the problem with that would be...?'

Her eyes widened as if he were talking crazy talk and a hard, heavy ball dropped into the pit of his stomach. It was all he could do not to bare his teeth and growl.

'I knew you wouldn't understand.'

'I'll tell you what I understand. That you're the most uptight, repressed person I have *ever* met.'

'Repressed?' Her mouth opened and closed. 'I— What are you doing?'

He'd seized her hand again and was towing her towards a copse of Aleppo pine and carob trees. 'What's that?' He flung an arm out at the vista spread below them.

She glared. 'The Aegean. It's beautiful.'

'And that?' He pointed upwards.

She followed his gaze. Frowned and shrugged,

evidently not following where he was going with this. 'The...sky?'

'The sun,' he snapped out. 'And it's shining in full force in case you hadn't noticed. And where are we?'

She swallowed. 'On a Greek island.'

He crowded her in against a tree, his arms going either side of her to block her in. 'If there was ever a time to let your hair down and rebel against your prim and proper strictures, Audra, now's the time to do it.'

She stared up at him with wide eyes, and he relished the moment—her stupefaction...her bewilderment...her undeniable hunger when her gaze lowered to his lips. This moment had seemed inevitable from when she'd appeared on the stairs a week ago to peer at him with those icy blue eyes, surveyed him in handcuffs, and told him it served him right.

His heart thudded against his ribs, he relished the adrenaline that surged through his body, before he swooped down to capture her lips in a kiss designed to shake up her safe little world. And he poured all his wildness and adventurous temptation into it in a devil-may-care invitation to dance.

CHAPTER EIGHT

THE ASSAULT ON Audra's senses the moment Finn's lips touched hers was devastating. She hadn't realised she could feel a kiss in so many ways, that its impact would spread through her in ever-widening circles that went deeper and deeper.

Finn's warmth beat at her like the warmth of the sun after a dip in the sea. It melted things that had been frozen for a very long time.

His scent mingled with the warm tang of the trees and sun-kissed grasses, and with just the tiniest hint of salt on the air it was exactly what a holiday should smell like. It dared her to play, it tempted her to reckless fun…and…and to a youthful joy she'd never allowed herself to feel before.

And she was powerless to resist. She had no defences against a kiss like this. It didn't feel as if defences were necessary. A kiss like this…it should be embraced and relished…welcomed.

Finn had been angry with her, but he didn't

kiss angry. He kissed her as though he couldn't help it—as though he'd been fighting a losing battle and had finally flung himself wholeheartedly into surrender. It was *intoxicating*.

Totally heady and wholly seductive.

She lifted her hands, but didn't know what to do with them so rested them on his shoulders, but they moved, restless, to the heated skin of his neck, and the skin-on-skin contact sent electricity coursing through both of them. He shuddered, she gasped…tongues tangled.

And then his arms were around her, hauling her against his body, her arms were around his neck as she plastered herself to him, and she stopped thinking as desire and the moment consumed her.

It was the raucous cry of a rose-ringed parakeet that penetrated her senses—and the need for air that had them easing apart. She stared into his face and wondered if her lips looked as well kissed as his, and if her eyes were just as dazed.

And then he swore, and a sick feeling crawled through the pit of her stomach. He let her go so fast she had to brace herself against the trunk of the tree behind her. She ached in places both familiar and unfamiliar and…and despite the myriad emotions chasing across his face—and none of them were positive—she wished with all her might that they were somewhere private, and that she were back in his arms so those aches could be assuaged.

And to hell with the consequences.

'I shouldn't have done that,' he bit out. 'I'm sorry.'

'I don't want an apology.'

The words left her without forethought, and with a brutal honesty that made her cringe. But they both knew what she *did* want couldn't happen. Every instinct she had told her he was hanging by a thread. His chest rose and fell as if he'd been running. The pulse at the base of his throat pounded like a mad thing. He wanted her with the same savage fury that she wanted him. And everything inside her urged her to snap his thread of control, and the consequences be damned.

It was *crazy*! Her hands clenched. She couldn't go on making romantic mistakes like this. Oh, he was nothing like Thomas. He'd never lie to her or betray her, but…but if she had an affair with Finn, it'd hurt her family. They'd see her as just another in a long line of Finn's *women*. It wasn't fair, but it was the reality all the same. She wouldn't hurt her family for the world; especially after all they'd been through with Thomas. She couldn't let them down so badly.

If she and Finn started something, when it ended—and that was the inevitable trajectory to all of Finn's relationships—he'd have lost her family's good opinion. They'd shun him. She knew how much that'd hurt him, and she'd do anything to prevent that from happening too.

And yet if he kissed her again she'd be lost.

'I'm not the person I thought I was,' she blurted out.

He frowned. 'What do you mean?'

Anger came to her rescue then. 'You wanted me to lose control. You succeeded in making that happen.' She moved in close until the heat from their bodies mingled again. 'And now you want me to just what…? Put it all back under wraps? To forget about it? What kind of game are you playing, Finn?'

The pulse in his jaw jumped and jerked. 'I just wanted you to loosen up a bit. Live in the moment instead of overthinking and over-analysing everything and…'

She slammed her hands to her hips. 'And?' She wasn't sure what she wanted from him—what she wanted him to admit—but it was more than this. That kiss had changed *everything*. But she wasn't even sure what that meant. Or what to do about it.

'And I'm an idiot! It was a stupid thing to do.' His eyes snapped fire as if *he* were angry with *her*. 'I do flings, Audra. Nothing more.' Panic lit his face. 'But I don't do them with Rupert's little sister.'

The car keys sailed through the air. She caught them automatically.

'I'll see you back at the villa.'

She watched as he stormed down the hill. He was running scared. From her? From fear of destroying his friendship with Rupert? Or was it something else...like thoughts of babies and marriage?

Was that what he thought she wanted from him?

Her stomach did a crazy twirl and she had to sit on a nearby rock to catch her breath. She'd be crazy to pin those kinds of hopes on him. And while she might be crazy with lust, she hadn't lost her mind completely.

She touched her fingers to her lips. *Oh, my, but the man could kiss.*

Audra glanced up from her spot on the sofa when Finn finally came in. She'd had dinner a couple of hours ago. She'd started to wonder if Finn meant to stay out all night.

And then she hadn't wanted to follow that thought any further, hadn't wanted to know where he might be and with whom…and what they might be doing.

He halted when he saw her. The light from the doorway framed him in exquisite detail—outlining the broad width of his shoulders and the lean strength of his thighs. Every lusty, heady impulse that had fired through her body when they'd kissed earlier fired back to life now, making her itch and yearn.

'I want to tell you something.'

He moved into the room, his face set and the lines bracketing his mouth deep. She searched him for signs of exhaustion, over-exertion, a limp, as he moved towards an armchair, but his body, while held tight, seemed hale and whole. Whatever else he'd done—or hadn't done—today, he clearly hadn't aggravated his recent injuries.

She let out a breath she hadn't even known she'd been holding. 'Okay.' She closed her book and set her feet to the floor. Here it came—the 'it's not you it's me' speech, the 'I care about you, but…' justifications. She tried to stop her lips from twisting. She'd toyed with a lot of scenarios since their kiss…and this was one of them. She had no enthusiasm for it. Perhaps it served her right for losing her head so completely earlier. A penance. She bit back a sigh. 'What do you want to tell me?'

'I want to explain why it's so important to me that I don't break Rupert's trust.'

That was easy. 'He's your best friend.' He cared more for Rupert than he did for her. It made perfect sense, so she couldn't explain why the knowledge chafed at her.

'I want you to understand how much I actually owe him.'

'How you *owe* him?' Would it be rude to get up, wish him goodnight and go to bed?'

Of course it'd be rude.

Not as rude as sashaying over to where he sat, planting herself in his lap, and kissing him.

She tried to close her mind to the pictures that exploded behind her eyelids. How many times did she have to tell herself that he was off limits?

'I haven't told another living soul about this and I suspect Rupert hasn't either.'

Her eyes sprang open. 'Okay. I'm listening.'

His eyes throbbed, but he stared at the wall behind her rather than at her directly. It made her chest clench. 'Finn?'

His nostrils flared. 'I went off the rails for a while when we were at school. I don't know if you know that or not.'

She shook her head.

'I was seventeen—full of hormones and angry at the world. I took to drinking and smoking and…and partying hard.'

With girls? She said nothing.

'I was caught breaking curfew twice…and one of those times I was drunk.'

She winced. 'That wouldn't have gone down well. Your boarding school was pretty strict.'

'With an excellent reputation to uphold. I was told in no uncertain terms that one more strike and I was out.'

She waited. 'So…? Rupert helped you clean up your act?'

'Audra, Audra, Audra.' His lips twisted into a mockery of a smile. 'You should know better than that.'

Her stomach started to churn, though she wasn't sure why. 'You kept pushing against the boundaries and testing the limits.'

He nodded.

'And were you caught?'

'Contraband was found in my possession.'

'What kind of contraband?'

'The type that should've had me automatically expelled.'

She opened her mouth and then closed it. It might be better not to know. 'But you weren't expelled.' Or had he been and somehow it'd all been kept a secret?

'No.'

The word dropped from him, heavy and dull, and all of the fine hairs on her arms lifted. 'How...?'

'Remember the Fallonfield Prize?'

She snorted. 'How could I not? Rupert was supposed to have been the third generation of Russel men to win that prize. I swear to God it was the gravest disappointment of both my father's and grandfather's lives when he didn't.'

Nobody had been able to understand it, because Rupert had been top of his class, and that, combined with his extra-curricular community service activities and demonstrated leadership skills...

Her throat suddenly felt dry. 'He was on track to win it.'

Finn nodded.

Audra couldn't look away. The Fallonfield

Prize was a prestigious award that opened doors. It practically guaranteed the winner a place at their university of choice, and it included a year-long mentorship with a business leader and feted humanitarian. As a result of winning the prize, her grandfather had gone to Chile for a year. Her father had gone to South Africa, which was where he'd met Audra's mother, who'd been doing aid work there. The Russel family's legacy of social justice and responsibility continued to this very day. Rupert had planned to go to Nicaragua.

'What happened?' she whispered, even though she could see the answer clear and plain for herself.

'Rupert took the blame. He said the stuff belonged to him, and that he'd stowed it among my things for safekeeping—so his parents wouldn't see it when they'd come for a recent visit.'

She moistened her lips. 'He had to know it'd cost him the scholarship.'

Finn nodded. He'd turned pale in the telling of the story and her heart burned for him. He'd lost his father when he was far too young, and then he'd watched his mother die. Who could blame him for being angry?

But… 'I'm amazed you—' She snapped her mouth closed. *Shut up!*

His lips twisted. 'You're amazed I let him take the rap?'

She swallowed and didn't say a word.

'I wasn't going to. When I'd found out what he'd done I started for the head's office to set him straight.'

'What happened?'

'Your brother punched me.'

'Rupert…' Her jaw dropped. Rupert had punched Finn?

'We had a set-to like I've never had before or since.'

She wanted to close her eyes.

'We were both bloody and bruised by the end of it, and when I was finally in a state to listen he grabbed me by the throat and told me I couldn't disappoint my uncle or your parents by getting myself kicked out of school—that I owed it to everyone and that I'd be a hundred different kinds of a weasel if I let you all down. He told me I wasn't leaving him there to cope with the fallout on his own. He told me I wasn't abandoning him to a life of stolid respectability. And…'

'And?' she whispered.

'And I started to cry like a goddamn baby.'

Her heart thumped and her chest ached.

'I'd felt so alone until that moment, and Rupert hugged me and called me his brother.'

Audra tried to check the tears that burned her eyes.

'He gave me a second chance. And make no mistake, if he hadn't won me that second chance I'd probably be dead now.'

Even through the haze of her tears, the ferocity of his gaze pierced her.

'He made me feel a part of something—a family, a community—where what I did mattered. And that made me turn my life around, made me realise that what I did had an impact on the people around me, that it mattered to somebody… that what I did with my life mattered.'

'Of course it matters.' He just hadn't been able to see that then.

'So I let him take the rap for me, knowing what it would cost him.'

She nodded, swiped her fingers beneath her eyes. 'I'm glad he did what he did. I'm glad you let him do it.' She understood now how much he must feel he owed Rupert.

'So when Rupert asks me to…to take care with his little sister, I listen.'

She stilled. Her heart gave a sick thump.

'I promised him that I wouldn't mess with you and your emotions. And I mean to keep my word.'

She stiffened. Nobody—not Rupert, not Finn—had any right to make such decisions on her behalf.

His eyes flashed. 'You owe me a "truth or dare" question.'

She blinked, taken off guard by the snap and crackle of his voice, by the way his lips had thinned. 'Fine. Ask your question.'

'Knowing what you know now, would you choose to destroy my friendship with Rupert for a quick roll in the hay, Squirt?'

He knew he was being deliberately crude and deliberately brutal, but he had to create some serious distance between him and Audra before he did something he'd regret for the rest of his life.

She rose, as regal as a queen, her face cold and her eyes chips of ice. 'I'd never do anything to hurt your friendship with Rupert. Whether I'd heard that story or not.'

And yet they'd both been tempted to earlier.

'So, Finn, you don't need to worry your pretty little head over that any longer.'

He had to grind his teeth together at her deliberately patronising tone.

She spun away. 'I'm going to bed.'

She turned in the doorway. 'Also, the name is Audra—not Squirt. Strike Two.'

With that she swept from the room. Finn fell back into his chair and dragged both hands through his hair. He should never have kissed her. He hadn't known that a kiss could rock the very foundations of his world in the way his kiss with Audra had. Talk about pride coming before a fall. The gods punished hubris, didn't they? He'd really thought he could kiss her and remain unmarked…unmoved…untouched.

The idea seemed laughable now.

He'd wanted to fling her out of herself and force her to act on impulse. He hadn't known he'd lose control. He hadn't known that kiss would fling him out of himself…and then return him as a virtual stranger.

If it'd been any other woman, he'd have not been able to resist following that kiss through to its natural conclusion, the consequences be damned. His mouth dried. Whatever else they were, he knew those consequences would've been significant. Maybe he and Audra had dodged a bullet.

Or maybe they'd—

Maybe nothing! He didn't do long term. He didn't do family and babies. He did fun and adventure and he kept things uncomplicated and simple. Because that was the foundation his life had been built on. It was innate, inborn… intrinsic to who he was. There were some things in this world you couldn't change. Leopards couldn't change their spots and Finn Sullivan couldn't change his freewheeling ways.

Finn heard Audra moving about in the kitchen the next morning, but he couldn't look up from the final pages of his book.

He read the final page…closed the cover.

Damn!

He stormed out into the kitchen and slammed the book to the counter. The split second after he'd done it, he winced and waited for her to jump out of her skin—waited for his stomach to curdle with self-loathing. He was such an idiot. He should've taken more care, but she simply looked at him, one eyebrow almost raised.

He nodded. 'Keep practising, it's almost there.'

She ignored that to glance at the book. 'Finished?'

He pointed at her and then slammed his finger

to the book. 'That was a dirty, rotten, low-down trick. It's not finished!'

'My understanding is that particular story arc concludes.'

'Yeah, but I don't know if he gets his kingdom back. I don't know if she saves the world and defeats the bad guy. And…and I don't know if they end up together!'

Both her eyebrows rose.

'You…you tricked me!'

She leaned across and pointed. 'It says it's a trilogy here… And it says that it's Book One here. I wasn't keeping anything from you.'

Hot damn. So it did. He just… He hadn't paid any attention to the stuff on the cover. He rocked back on his heels, hands on hips. 'Didn't see that,' he murmured. 'And I really want to know how it ends.'

'And you feel cheated because you have to read another two books to find that out?'

Actually, the idea should appal him. But… 'I, uh…just guess I'm impatient to know how it all works out.'

'That's easily fixed. The bookshop in the village has the other two books in stock.'

He shoved his hands into his back pockets. 'Sorry, I shouldn't have gone off like that. Just didn't know what I was signing up for when I started the book.'

'God, Finn!' She took a plate of sliced fruit to the table and sat. 'That's taking commitment phobia to a whole new level.'

He indicated her plate. 'I'm supposed to do breakfast. That was part of the deal.'

'Part of the deal was calling me Audra too.'

She lifted a piece of melon to her lips. He tried to keep his face smooth, tried to keep his pulse under control as her mouth closed about the succulent fruit. 'So…what's on the agenda today?'

She ate another slice of melon before meeting his gaze. 'I want a Finn-free day.'

He fought the automatic urge to protest. An urge he knew was crazy because a day spent not in each other's company would probably be a wise move. 'Okay.'

'I bags the beach this morning.'

It took all his strength to stop from pointing out it was a long beach with room enough for both of them.

'Why don't you take the car and go buy your books, and then go do something you'd consider fun?'

Lying on a beach, swimming and reading a book, those things were fun. He rolled his shoulders. So were jetskiing and waterskiing and stuff. 'Okay.' He thrust out his jaw. 'Sounds great.'

She rose and rinsed her plate. 'And you'll have the house to yourself this evening.'

Her words jolted him up to his full height. 'Why?'

'Because I'm going into the village for a meal, and maybe some dancing. *Not* that it's any of your business.'

She wanted to go dancing? 'I'll take you out if that's what you want.'

'No, thank you, Finn.'

'But—'

Her eyes sparked. 'I don't want to go out to dinner or dancing with you.'

'Why not?' The words shot out of him and he immediately wished them back.

She folded her arms and peered down her nose at him. 'Do you really want me to answer that?'

He raised his hands and shook his head, but the anger in her eyes had his mind racing. 'You're annoyed with me. Because I kissed you?' Or because he wouldn't kiss her again?

Stop thinking about kissing her.

'Oh, I'm livid with you.'

He swallowed.

'And with Rupert.'

He stiffened. 'What's Rupert done? He's not even here.'

'And with myself.' She folded her arms, her expression more bewildered than angry now. 'You really don't see it, do you?'

See what?

'Between you, you and Rupert decided what was in my best interests. And—' the furrow in her brow deepened '—I let you. I went along with it instead of pointing out how patronising and controlling it was.' She lifted her chin. 'I'm a grown-up who has the right to make her own choices and decisions, be they wise or unwise. I'm not a child. I don't need looking after, and I do *not* have to consult with either of you if I want to kiss someone or...or start a relationship. And that's why I'm going into the village this evening on my own without an escort—to remind myself that I'm an adult.'

She swept up her beach bag and her sunhat and stalked out of the door.

I do not *have to consult...if I want to kiss someone...*

Was she planning on kissing someone tonight? But...but she couldn't.

Why not?

Scowling, he slammed the frying pan on a hot

plate, turned it up to high before throwing in a couple of rashers of bacon. He cracked in two eggs as well. Oops—fine, he'd have scrambled eggs. He ground his teeth together. He *loved* scrambled eggs.

He gathered up the litter to throw into the bin, pushed open the lid…and then stilled. Setting the litter down on the counter again, he pulled out three A4 sheets of paper from the bottom of the bin, wiped off the fruit skins and let forth a very rude word. These were his designs for Audra's shop. He glared out of the glass sliding doors, but Audra had disappeared from view. 'That's not going to work, Princess.'

He pulled the frying pan from the heat, went to his room to grab his laptop and then strode into Rupert's office, heading straight for the printer.

He placed one set of printouts on the coffee table. The next set he placed on the tiny hall table outside her bedroom door. The third set he put in a kitchen drawer. The next time she reached for the plastic wrap, they'd greet her. The rest he kept in a pile in his bedroom to replace any of the ones she threw away.

'You're not taking the car?'

Audra didn't deign to answer him.

He glanced at his watch. 'Six thirty is a bit early for dinner, isn't it?'

She still didn't answer him. She simply peered at her reflection in the foyer mirror, and slicked on another coat of ruby-red lipstick. Utter perfection. She wore a sundress that made his mouth water too—the bodice hugged her curves, showing off a delectable expanse of golden skin at her shoulders and throat while the skirt fell in a floaty swirl of aqua and scarlet to swish about her calves. His heart pounded.

Don't think about messing up that lipstick.

He shoved his hands into his pockets. 'Why aren't you taking the car?'

She finally turned. 'Because I plan to have a couple of drinks. And I don't drink and drive.'

'But how will you get home?'

She raised an eyebrow.

He raised one back at her. 'You've almost got that down pat.'

She waved a hand in front of her face. 'Stop it, Finn.'

'What? It was a compliment and—'

'Stop it with the twenty questions. I know what time I want to eat. I know how to get home at the end of an evening out. Or—' she smiled, but it didn't reach eyes that flashed and sparked

'—how to get home the morning after an evening out if that's the way the evening rocks.'

She…she might not be coming home? But—

And then she was gone in a swirl of perfume and red and aqua skirt as the village taxi pulled up in the driveway and tooted its horn.

Finn spent the evening pacing. Audra might be a grown woman, but she'd had fire in her eyes as she'd left. He knew she was angry with him and Rupert, but what if that anger led her to do something stupid…something she'd later regret? What the hell would he tell Rupert if something happened to her?

He lasted until nine p.m. Jumping in the car, it felt like a relief to finally be doing something, to be setting off after her. Not that he knew what he was going to do once he did find her.

She was in the first place he looked—Petra's Taverna. The music pouring from its open windows and doors was lively and cheerful. Tables spilled onto the courtyard outside and down to a tiny beach. Finn chose a table on the edge of the scene in the shadows of a cypress with an excellent view, via two enormous windows, inside the taverna.

Audra drew his eyes like a magnet. She sat on a stool framed in one of the windows and threw her head back at something her companion said, though Finn's view of her companion was blocked. She nodded and her companion came into view—a handsome young local—as they moved to the dance floor.

Beneath the table, Finn's hands clenched. When a waiter came he ordered a lemon squash. Someone had to keep their wits about them this evening! As the night wore on, Finn's scowl only grew and it deterred anyone who might've been tempted from coming across and trying to engage him in conversation.

And the more morose he grew, the merrier the tabloid inside became. As if those two things were related.

Audra was the life of the party. He lost track of the number of dance partners she had. She laughed and talked with just about every person in the taverna. She alternated glasses of white wine with big glasses of soda water. She snacked on olives and crisps and even played a hand of cards. She charmed everyone. And everything charmed her. He frowned. He'd not realised before how popular she was here in Kyanós. His frown deepened. It struck him that she was more alive here than he could ever remember seeing her.

And at a little after midnight, and after many pecks on cheeks were exchanged, she caught the taxi—presumably back to the villa—on her own.

He sat there feeling like an idiot. She'd had an evening out—had let her hair down and had some fun. She hadn't drunk too much. She hadn't flirted outrageously and hadn't needed to fight off inappropriate advances. She hadn't done anything foolish or reckless or ill-considered. She hadn't needed him to come to her rescue.

I'm a grown-up who has the right to make her own choices.

And what was he? Not just a fool, but some kind of creep—a sneak spying on a woman because he'd been feeling left out and unnecessary. And as far as Audra was concerned, he *was* unnecessary. *Completely* unnecessary. She didn't need him.

He could try to dress it up any way he liked—that he'd been worried about her, that he wanted to make sure she stayed safe—but what he'd done was spy on her and invade her privacy.

Why the hell had he done that? What right did he think he had?

Earlier she'd accused him and Rupert of being patronising and controlling, and she was right.

She deserved better from him. Much better.

CHAPTER NINE

WHEN AUDRA REACHED in the fridge for the milk for her morning coffee and found yet another set of printouts—in a plastic sleeve, no less, that would presumably protect them from moisture and condensation—it was all she could do not to scream.

She and Finn had spent the last three days avoiding each other. She'd tried telling herself that suited her just fine, but...

It *should* suit her just fine. She had the beach to herself in the mornings, while Finn took the car and presumably headed into the village. And then he had the beach in the afternoons while she commandeered the car. In terms of avoiding each other, it worked *perfectly*. It was just...

She blew out a breath. She wished avoidance tactics weren't necessary. She wished they could go back to laughing and having fun and teasing each other as they had before that stupid kiss.

And before she'd got all indignant about Rupert's overprotectiveness, and galled that Finn had unquestioningly fallen into line with it…and angry with herself for not having challenged it earlier. Where once her brother's protectiveness had made her feel cared for, now it left her feeling as if she was a family liability who needed safeguarding against her own foolishness.

Because of Thomas?

Or because if she could no longer hold tight to the label of being responsible and stable then… then what could she hold onto?

Stop it! Of course she was still responsible and stable. Thomas had been a mistake, and everyone was entitled to one mistake, right? Just as long as she didn't compound that by doing something stupid with Finn; just as long as she maintained a sense of responsibility and calm and balance, and remembered who *he* was and remembered who *she* was.

Sloshing milk into her coffee, she went to throw the printouts in the bin when her gaze snagged on some subtle changes to the pictures. Curiosity warred with self-denial. Curiosity won. Grabbing a croissant—Finn always made sure there was a fresh supply—she slipped outside to the picnic table to pore over the designs of this achingly and heart-wrenchingly beautiful shop.

Letting her hair down and doing things she

wanted to do just for the sake of it—for fun—hadn't helped the burning in her soul whenever she was confronted with these pictures. They were snapshots of a life she could never have. And with each fresh reminder—and for some reason Finn seemed hell-bent on reminding her—that burn scorched itself into her deeper and deeper.

She bit into the croissant, she sipped coffee, but she tasted nothing.

Ever since Finn had kissed her she'd...*wanted.*

She'd *wanted* to kiss him again. She wanted *more.* She'd not known that a kiss could fill you with such a physical need. That it could make you crave so hard. She was twenty-seven years old. She'd thought she knew about attraction. She'd had good sex before. But that kiss had blown her preconceptions out of the stratosphere. And it had left her floundering. Because there was no way on God's green earth that she and Finn could go *there.* She didn't doubt that in the short term it'd be incredible, but ultimately it'd be destructive. She wasn't going to be responsible for that kind of pain—for wounding friendships and devastating family ties and connections.

She couldn't do that to Rupert.

She wouldn't do that to Finn.

But the kiss had left her wanting *more* from life too. And she didn't know how to make that restlessness and sense of dissatisfaction go away.

So she'd tried a different strategy in the hope it would help. Instead of reining in all her emotions and desires, she'd let a few of them loose. Finn was right: if there was ever a time to rebel it was now when she was on holiday. She'd hoped a mini-rebellion would help her deal with her attraction for Finn. She'd hoped it would help her deal with the dreary thought of returning home to her job.

She'd gone dancing. It'd been fun.

She'd taken an art class and had learned about form and perspective. Her drawing had been terrible, but moving a pencil across paper had soothed her. The focus of next week's class was going to be composition. Her shoulders sagged. Except she wouldn't be here next week.

She'd even gone jetskiing again. It'd felt great to be zipping across the water. But no sooner had she returned the jetski than her restlessness had returned.

She pressed her hands to her face and then pulled them back through her hair. She'd hoped those things would help ease the ache in her soul, but they hadn't. They'd only fed it. It had been a mistake to come here.

And she wished to God Finn had never kissed her!

'Morning, Audra.'

As if her thoughts had conjured him, Finn appeared. His wide grin and the loose easy way he settled on the seat opposite with a bowl of cereal balanced in one hand inflamed her, though she couldn't have said why. She flicked the offending printouts towards him. 'Why are you leaving these all over the house?'

He ate a spoonful of cereal before gesturing to them. 'Do you like the changes I've made?'

'I—'

'Market research suggests that locating the point of sale over here provides for "a more comfortable retail experience"—' he made quotation marks in the air with one hand '—for the customer.'

She had to physically refrain from reaching across and shaking him. Drawing in a breath, she tried to channel responsible, calm balance. 'Why does any of this matter?'

'Because it needs to be perfect.'

Her chest clenched. Her eyes burned. Balance fled. 'Why?'

He shrugged and ate more cereal. 'Because that's what I do. I create designs as near perfect as possible.'

Didn't he know what these pictures and the constant reminders were doing to her?

He pulled the sheets from their plastic sleeve. 'What do you think about this shelving arrangement? It's neither better nor more functional than the ones you've already chosen, but apparently this design is all the range in Scandinavia at the moment, so I thought I'd throw it into the mix just to see what you thought?'

She couldn't help it; she had to look. The sleek lines were lovely, but these didn't fit in with the overall feel she was trying to achieve at all.

You're not trying to achieve an overall feel, remember? Pipe dream!

With a growl she slapped the picture facedown.

'No?' He raised one eyebrow—perfectly— which set her teeth even further on edge. 'Fair enough.'

'Enough already,' she countered through gritted teeth. 'Stop plastering these designs all over the house. I've had enough. I can see you do good work—excellent work. I'm sorry I misjudged you, but I believe I've already apologised.

I'll apologise again if you need me to. But stop with the pictures. *Please.*'

He abandoned his breakfast to lean back and stare at her. She couldn't help wondering what he saw—a repressed woman he'd like to muss up?

It was what she wanted to believe. If it were true it'd provide her with a form of protection. But it wasn't true. She knew that kiss had shaken him as much as it'd shaken her. It was why he'd avoided her for these last few days as assiduously as she had him.

'I'll stop with the pictures of the shop if you answer one question for me.'

'Oh, here we go again.' She glared. She didn't raise an eyebrow. She needed more practice before she tried that again. She folded her arms instead. 'Ask your question.'

He leaned towards her. The perfect shape of his mouth had a sigh rising up through her. 'Why are you working as an operations manager instead of opening up your dream shop here on this island and living a life that makes you happy?'

She flinched. His words were like an axe to her soul. How did he know? When Rupert, Cora and Justin had no idea? When she'd been so careful that none of them should know?

He held up the printouts and shook them at

her. 'Your face when you described this shop, Audra… You came alive. It was…'

Her heart thumped so hard she could barely breathe.

'Magnificent,' he finally decided. 'And catching.'

She blinked. 'Catching…how?'

'Contagious! Your enthusiasm was contagious. I've not felt that enthusiastic about anything—'

He broke off with a frown. '—for a long time,' he finished. He stared at each of the three pictures. 'I want you to have this shop. I want you to have this life. I don't understand why you're punishing yourself.'

Her head reared back. 'I'm not punishing myself.'

'I'm sorry, Princess, but that's not what it looks like from where I'm sitting.'

'I do worthy work!' She shot to her feet, unable to sit for the agitation roiling through her. 'The work the Russel Corporation does is important.' She strode across to the bluff to stare out at the turquoise water spread below.

'I'm not disputing that.' His voice came from just behind her. 'But…so what?'

She spun to face him. 'How can you say that?

Look at the amazing things Rupert, Cora and Justin are doing.'

His jaw dropped. 'This is about sibling rivalry? Come on, Audra, you're twenty-seven years old. I know you always wanted to keep up with the others when you were younger, but—' He scanned her face, rocked back on his heels. 'It's not about sibling rivalry.'

'No,' she said. It was about sibling loyalty. *Family* loyalty.

He remained silent, just…waiting.

She pressed her fingers to her temples for a moment before letting her arms drop back to her sides. 'When our mother died it felt like the end of the world.'

He reached out and closed his hand around hers and she suddenly felt less alone, less… diminished. She gripped his hand and stared doggedly out to sea. She couldn't look at him. If she looked at him she might cry. 'She was the lynchpin that kept all our worlds turning. The crazy thing was I never realised that until she was gone.' She hauled in a breath. 'And the work she did at the Russel Corporation was crucial.'

Karen Russel had been the administrator of the Russel Corporation's charity arm, and Audra's father had valued her in that role without reservation. Humanitarian endeavours formed a key component of the corporation's mission statement and it wasn't one he was comfortable trusting to anyone outside the family.

'But her influence was so much wider than that.' She blinked against the sting in her eyes. 'She worked out a strategy for Rupert to evolve into the role of CEO; she researched laboratories that would attract the most funding and would therefore provide Cora with the most promising opportunities. If she'd lived long enough she'd have found excellent funding for Justin's efforts in South-East Asia.' Justin was implementing a dental-health programme to the impoverished populations in Cambodia. He had ambitions to take his programme to all communities in need throughout South-East Asia.

She felt him turn towards her. 'Instead you found those funding opportunities for him. You should be proud of yourself.'

No sooner were the words out of his mouth than he stilled. She couldn't look at him. He swore softly. 'Audra—'

'When our mother died, I'd never seen the rest of my family so devastated.' She shook her hand free. 'I wanted to make things better for them.

You should've seen my father's relief when I said I'd take over my mother's role in the corporation after I'd finished university. Justin floundered towards the end of his last year of study. He had exams coming up but started panicking about the licences and paperwork he needed to file to work in Cambodia, and finding contacts there. The laboratory Cora worked for wanted sponsorship from business and expected her to approach the family corporation. And Rupert… well, he missed the others so having me around to boss helped.'

She'd stepped into the breach because Karen was no longer there to do it. And someone had to. It'd broken her heart to see her siblings hurting so badly.

Finn had turned grey. He braced his hands on his knees, and she couldn't explain why, but she had to swallow the lump that did everything it could to lodge in her throat. 'You've been what they've all needed you to be.'

'I'm not a martyr, Finn. I *love* my family. I'm proud I've been able to help.' Helping them had helped her to heal. It'd given her a focus, when her world had felt as if it were spinning out of control.

He straightened, his eyes dark. 'She wouldn't want this for you.'

'You don't know that.' She lifted her chin. 'I think she'd be proud of me.'

He chewed on his bottom lip, his brows lowering over his eyes. 'Have you noticed how each of you have coped with your mother's death in different ways?'

She blinked.

'Rupert became super-protective of you all.'

Rupert had always been protective, but… She nodded. He'd become excessively so since their mother's death.

'Cora threw herself into study. She wanted to top every class she took.'

Cora had found solace in her science textbooks.

'Justin started living more in the moment.'

She hadn't thought about it in those terms, but she supposed he had.

One corner of Finn's mouth lifted. 'Which means he leaves things to the last minute and relies on his little sister to help make them right.'

Her lips lifted too.

'While you, Princess…' He sobered. 'You've tried to fill the hole your mother has left behind.'

She shook her head. 'Only the practical day-to-day stuff.' Nobody could fill the emotional hole she'd left behind.

'Your siblings have a genuine passion for what they do, though. They're following their dreams.'

And in a small way she'd been able to facilitate that. She didn't regret that for a moment.

'You won't be letting your mother down if you follow your own dreams and open a shop here on Kyanós.'

'That's not what it feels like.' She watched a seabird circle and then dive into the water below. 'If I leave the Russel Corporation it'll feel as if I'm betraying them all.'

'You'll be the only who feels that way.'

The certainty in his tone had her swinging to him.

He lifted his hands to his head, before dropping them back to his sides. 'Audra, they're all doing work they love!'

'Good!' She stared at his fists and then into his face. He was getting really het-up about this. 'I want them to love what they do.'

'Then why don't you extend yourself that same courtesy?'

He bellowed the words, and her mouth opened and closed but no sound came out. He made it sound so easy. But it wasn't! She loved being there for her brothers and sister. She loved that she could help them.

'How would you feel if you discovered Rupert or Cora or Justin were doing their jobs just to keep you feeling comfortable and emotionally secure?'

Oh, that'd be awful! It'd—

She took a step away from him, swallowed. Her every muscle scrunched up tight. That scenario, it wasn't synonymous with hers.

Why not?

She pressed her hands to her cheeks, trying to cool them. Her siblings were each brilliant in their own way—fiercely intelligent, politically savvy and driven. She wasn't. Her dreams were so ordinary in comparison, so lacking in ambition. A part of her had always been afraid that her family would think she wasn't measuring up to her potential.

Her heart started to pound. Had she been using her role in the family corporation as an excuse to hide behind? Stretching her own wings required taking risks, and those risks frightened her.

'I hate to say this, Princess, but when you get right down to brass tacks you're just a glorified administrator, a pen-pusher, and anyone can do the job that you do.'

* * *

'Why don't you tell me what you really think, Finn?'

The stricken expression in Audra's eyes pierced straight through the centre of him. He didn't want to hurt her. But telling her what he really thought was wiser than doing what he really wanted to do, which was kiss her.

He had to remind himself again of all the reasons kissing her was a bad idea.

He pulled in a breath. He didn't want to hurt her. He wanted to see her happy. He wanted to see her happy the way she'd been happy when describing her shop...when she'd been learning to ride a jetski...and when she'd been dancing. Did she truly think those things were frivolous and self-indulgent?

He tapped a fist against his lips as he stared out at the glorious view spread in front of them. The morning sun tinged everything gold, not so much as a breeze ruffled the air and it made the water look otherworldly still, and soft, like silk and mercury.

He pulled his hand back to his side. *Right.* 'It's my day.'

From the corner of his eye he saw her turn towards him. 'Pardon?'

'To choose our activities. It's my day.'

She folded her arms and stuck out a hip. She was going to tell him to go to blazes—that she was spending the day *on her own*. She opened her mouth, but he rushed on before she could speak. 'There's something I want to show you.'

She snapped her mouth shut, but her gaze slid over him as if it couldn't help it, and the way she swallowed and spun seawards again, her lips parted as if to draw much-needed air into her lungs, had his skin drawing tight. She was right. It'd be much wiser to continue to avoid each other.

But...

But he might never get this opportunity again. He wanted to prove to her that she had a right to be happy, to urge her to take that chance.

'The yacht with the pink and blue sail is back.'

She pointed but he didn't bother looking. 'Please,' he said quietly.

She met his gaze, her eyes searching his, before she blew out a breath and shrugged. 'Okay. Fine.'

'Dress code is casual and comfortable. We're not hiking for miles or doing anything gruelling. I just... I've been exploring and I think I've found some things that will interest you.'

'Sunhat and sandals…?'

'Perfect. How soon can you be ready?'

One slim shoulder lifted. 'Half an hour.'

'Excellent.' He gathered up his breakfast things and headed back towards the house before he did something stupid like kiss her.

Their first port of call was Angelo's workshop. Angelo was a carpenter who lived on the far side of the village. He made and sold furniture from his renovated garage. Most of the pieces he made were too large for Audra's hypothetical shop— chest of drawers, tables and chairs, bedheads and bookcases—but there were some smaller items Finn knew she'd like, like the pretty trinket boxes and old-fashioned writing desks that were designed to sit on one's lap.

As he'd guessed, Audra was enchanted. She ran a finger along a pair of bookends. 'The workmanship is exquisite.'

Finn nodded. 'He says that each individual piece of wood that he works with tells him what it wants to be.'

'You've spoken to him?'

'Finn!' Angelo rushed into the garage. 'I thought that was your car out front. Come, you and Audra must have coffee with the family. Maria has just made *baklava*.'

'Angelo!' Audra gestured around the room. 'I didn't know you made such beautiful things.'

Finn stared at her. 'You know Angelo?'

'Of course! His brother Petros is Rupert's gardener. And Maria used to work in the bakery.'

They stayed an hour.

Next Finn took Audra to Anastasia's studio, which sat solitary on a windswept hill. He rolled his eyes. 'Now you're going to tell me you know Anastasia.'

She shook her head. 'I've not had that pleasure.'

Anastasia took Audra for a tour of her photography studio while Finn trailed along behind. If the expression on Audra's face was anything to go by, Anastasia's photographs transfixed her. They'd transfixed him too. It was all he could do to drag her back to the car when the tour was finished.

Then it was back into the village to visit Eleni's workshop, where she demonstrated how she made not only scented soap from products sourced locally, but a range of skincare and cosmetic products as well. Audra lifted a set of soaps in a tulle drawstring bag, the satin ribbon entwined with lavender and some other herbs Finn couldn't identify. 'These are packaged so prettily I can't resist.' She bought some candles too.

They visited a further two tradespeople—a leather worker who made wallets and purses, belts and ornately worked book jackets, and a jeweller. Audra came away with gifts for her entire family.

'Hungry?' he asked as he started the car. He'd walked this hill over the last three days, searching for distraction, but today, for the sake of efficiency, he'd driven.

'Starved.'

They headed back down the hill to the harbour, and ate a late lunch of *marida* and *spanakorizo* at a taverna that had become a favourite. They dined beneath a bougainvillea-covered pergola and watched as the water lapped onto the pebbled beach just a few metres away.

Audra broke the silence first. 'Anastasia's work should hang in galleries. It's amazing. Her photographs reveal a Greece so different from the tourist brochures.'

'She's seventy. She does everything the old way. She doesn't even have the internet.'

She nodded and sipped her wine, before setting her wine glass down with a click. 'I'd love for Isolde, one of my friends from school—she's an interior decorator and stager, furnishes houses and apartments so they look their absolute best for selling—to see some of Angelo's bigger pieces. She'd go into raptures over them.' She started to rise. 'We need to go back and take some photos so I can send her—'

'My *loukoumades* haven't come yet.' He waved her back to her seat. 'There's time. We can go back tomorrow.' He topped up her wine. 'What about Eleni's pretty smelly things? They'd look great in a shop.'

Audra shook her head and then nodded, as if holding a conversation with herself. 'I should put her in touch with Cora's old lab partner, Elise. Remember her? She moved into the cosmetic industry. Last I heard she was making a big push for eco-friendly products. I bet she'd love Eleni's recipes.'

She was still putting everyone else's needs before her own. The *loukoumades* came and a preoccupied Audra helped him eat them. While her attention was elsewhere, he couldn't help but feast his eyes on her. She'd put on a little weight over the last eleven days. She had colour in her cheeks and her eyes sparked with interest and vitality. An ache grew inside him until he could barely breathe.

He tried to shake it off. Under his breath he called himself every bad name he could think of. Did he really find the allure of the forbidden so hard to resist?

He clenched his jaw. He *would* resist. He'd cut off his right hand rather than let Rupert down. He'd cut off his entire arm rather than ever hurt Audra.

But when she came alive like this, he couldn't look away.

She slapped her hands lightly to the table. 'I wonder how the villagers would feel about an annual festival.'

'What kind of festival?'

'One that showcases the local arts and crafts scene, plus all the fresh produce available here— the cured meats, the cheeses, the olive oils and... and...'

'The *loukoumades*?'

'Definitely the *loukoumades*!'

She laughed. She hadn't laughed, not with him, since he'd kissed her...and the loss of that earlier intimacy had been an ache in his soul.

The thought that he might be able to recapture their earlier ease made his heart beat faster.

'What?' she said, touching her face, and he realised he was staring.

He forced himself backwards in his seat. 'You're amazing, you know that?'

Her eyes widened. 'Me?'

'Absolutely. Can't you see how well you'd fit in here, and what a difference you could make? You've connections, energy and vision…passion.'

She visibly swallowed at that last word, and he had to force his gaze from the line of her throat. He couldn't let it linger there or he'd be lost.

Her face clouded over. 'I can't just walk away from the Russel Corporation.'

'Why not?' He paused and then nodded. 'Okay, you can't leave *just like that*.' He snapped his fingers. 'You'd have to hang around long enough to train up your replacement…or recruit a replacement.'

He could see her overdeveloped sense of duty begin to overshadow her excitement at the possibilities life held for her. He refused to let it win. 'Can you imagine how much your mother would've enjoyed the festival you just described?'

Her eyes filled.

'I remember how much she used to enjoy the local market days on Corfu, back when the family used to holiday there…when we were all children,' he said. Karen Russel had been driven and focussed, but she'd relished her downtime too.

'I know. I just...' Audra glanced skywards and blinked hard. 'I'd just want her to be proud of me.'

Something twisted in Finn's chest. Karen had died at a crucial stage in Audra's life—when Audra had been on the brink of adulthood. She'd been tentatively working her way towards a path that would give her life purpose and meaning, and searching for approval and support from the woman she'd looked up to. Her siblings had all had that encouragement and validation, but it'd been cruelly taken from Audra. No wonder she'd lost her way. 'Princess, I can't see how she could be anything else.'

Blue eyes, swimming with uncertainty and remembered grief, met his.

'Audra, you're kind and you work hard. You love your family and are there for them whenever they need you. She valued those things. And I think she'd thank you from the bottom of her heart for stepping into the breach when she was gone and doing all the things that needed doing.'

A single tear spilled onto her cheek, and he had to blink hard himself.

'The thing is,' he forced himself to continue,

'nobody needs you to do those things any more. And I'd lay everything on the bet that your mother would have loved the shop you described to me. Look at the way she lived her life—with passion and with zeal. She'd want you to do the same.'

Audra swiped her fingers beneath her eyes and pulled in a giant breath. 'Can…can we walk for a bit?'

They walked along the harbour and Audra hooked her arm through his. The accidental brushing of their bodies as they walked was a sweet torture that made him prickle and itch and want, but she'd done it without thinking or forethought—as if she needed to be somehow grounded while her mind galloped at a million miles an hour. So he left it there and didn't pull away, and fought against the growing need that pounded through him.

She eventually released him to sit on the low harbour wall, and he immediately wanted to drag her hand back into the crook of his arm and press his hand over it to keep it there.

'So,' she started. 'You're saying it wouldn't be selfish of me to move here and open my shop?'

'That's exactly what I'm saying. I know you

can't see it, but you don't have a selfish bone in your body.'

Sceptical eyes lifted to meet his. 'You really don't think I'd be letting my family down if I did that?'

'Absolutely not. I think they'd be delighted for you.' He fell down beside her. 'But don't take my word for it. Ask them.'

She pondered his words and then frowned. 'Do you honestly think I could fit in and become a permanent part of the community here on Kyanós?'

He did, but... 'Don't you?' Because at the end of the day it wasn't about what he thought. It was what she thought and believed that mattered.

'I want to believe it,' she whispered, 'because I want so badly for it to be true. I'm afraid that's colouring my judgement.'

He remained silent.

'I don't have half the talents of the artisans we visited today.' She drummed her fingers against her thigh. 'But I do have pretty good admin and organisational skills. I know how to run a business. I have my savings.'

She pressed her hands to her stomach. 'And it'd be so exciting to showcase local arts and crafts in my shop—nobody else is doing that so

I'd not be going into competition with another business on the island. I'd be careful not to stock anything that was in direct competition with the bookshop or the clothing boutiques. And I could bring in some gorgeous bits and bobs that aren't available here.'

Her face started to glow. 'And if everyone else here thought it was a good idea, it'd be really fun to help organise a festival. All my friends would come. And maybe my family could take time off from their busy schedules.'

She leapt to her feet, paced up and down in front of him. 'I could do this.'

'You could. But the question is…'

She halted and leaned towards him. 'What's the question?'

He rested back on his hands. 'The question is, are you going to?'

Fire streaked through her eyes, making them sparkle more brilliantly than the water in the harbour. 'Uh-huh.' She thrust out her chin, and then a grin as wide as the sky itself spread across her face. And Finn felt as if he were scudding along on an air current, sailing through the sky on some euphoric cloud of warmth and possibility.

'I'm going to do it.'

She did a little dance on the spot. She grinned

at him as if she didn't know what else to do. And then she leaned forward and, resting her hands on his shoulders, kissed him. Her lips touched his, just for a moment. It was a kiss of elation and excitement—a kiss of thanks, a kiss between friends. And it was pure and magical, and it shifted the axis of Finn's world.

She eased away, her lips parted, her breath coming fast and her eyes dazed, the shock in her face no doubt reflecting the shock in his. She snatched her hands away, smoothed them down the sides of her skirt and it was as if the moment had never been.

Except he had a feeling it was branded on his brain for all time. Such a small contact shouldn't leave such an indelible impression.

'Thank you, Finn.'

He shook himself. 'I didn't do anything.'

She raised an eyebrow and then shook her head and collapsed back down beside him on the sea wall. 'Don't say anything. I know it needs more practice. And you did do something—something big. You helped me see things differently. You gave me the nudge I needed and…' She turned and met his gaze, her smile full of excitement. 'I'm going to change my life. I'm going to turn it upside down. And I can't wait.'

Something strange and at odds like satisfaction and loss settled in the pit of his stomach, warring with each other for pre-eminence. He stoutly ignored it to grin back and clap his hands. 'Right! This calls for champagne.'

CHAPTER TEN

AUDRA WOKE EARLY, and the moment her eyes opened she found herself grinning. She drummed her heels against the mattress with a silent squeal as her mind sparked and shimmered with plans and purpose.

She threw on some clothes and her running shoes, before picking her way down to the beach and starting to run.

To run.

Unlike the previous three mornings—when she and Finn had been avoiding each other—she didn't time herself. She ran because she had an excess of energy and it seemed a good idea to get rid of some of it. The decisions she was about to make would impact the rest of her life and, while joy and excitement might be driving her, she needed to make decisions based on sound business logic. She wanted this dream to last forever—not just until her money ran out and she'd bankrupted herself.

She reached the sheer wall of cliff at the beach's

far end and leaned against it, bracing her hands on her knees, her breath coming hard and fast. Who'd have thought she could run all this way? She let out a whoop. Who knew running could feel so *freeing*?

She pulled off her shoes and socks and ambled back along the shoreline, relishing the wash of cool water against her toes as she made her way back towards the villa.

When she walked in, Finn glanced up from where he slouched against the breakfast bar, mug of coffee clasped in one hand. His eyes widened as they roved over her. He straightened. 'Have you been for a run?'

Heat mounted her cheeks. 'I, uh…'

One side of his mouth hooked up in that grin, and her blood started to pound harder than when she'd been running. 'That's not a "truth or dare" question, Audra. A simple yes or no will suffice.'

She dropped her shoes to the floor and helped herself to coffee. 'You got me kind of curious when you wanted us to run that day.' He'd made her feel like a lazy slob, but she didn't say that out loud because she didn't want him to feel bad about that. Not after everything he'd done for her yesterday. 'Made me wonder if I *could* run the length of the beach.'

'I bet you rocked it in.'

His faith warmed her. 'Not *rocked* it in,' she confessed, planting herself at the table. 'But I did it. And it gets a bit easier every day.'

He moved to sit opposite. 'You've been for more than one run? How many?'

She rolled her shoulders. 'Only four.'

'And you don't hate it?'

'It's not like my new favourite thing or anything.' But she didn't *hate* it. Sometimes it felt good to be pounding along the sand. It made her feel…powerful. 'I like having done it. It makes me feel suitably virtuous.'

He laughed and pointed to a spot above her head. 'That's one very shiny halo.'

He leaned back and drained his coffee. 'Who'd have thought it? You find you don't hate running, and I find I don't hate lying on a beach reading a book.'

He hadn't seemed restless for any of his usual hard and fast sports. She opened her mouth to ask him about it, but closed it again. She didn't want to put ideas into his head.

He rose. 'I had a couple of new thoughts about some designs for your shop. Wanna see them after breakfast?'

That caught her attention. 'Yes, please!'

An hour later she sat at the outdoor picnic table with Finn, soaking up the sun, the views and the incredible designs he kept creating. 'These are amazing.' She pulled his laptop closer towards her. 'You've gone into so much detail.'

'You gave me good material to work with.'

She flicked through the images he'd created, loving everything that she saw. 'You said—that first day when you showed me what you did— that the first step was the "dreaming big with no holds barred" step.'

He nodded.

She pulled in a breath. 'What's the next step?'

'Ah.' His lips twisted. 'The next step consists of the far less sexy concept of compromise.'

'Compromise?'

He pointed towards his computer. 'These are the dream, but what are the exact physical dimensions of your shop going to be? We won't know that until you find premises and either buy them or sign a lease. So these designs would have to be modified to fit in with that.'

Right.

'You'll also need to take into account any building works that may need doing on these new premises. And if so, what kind of council approvals you might need. Does the building have any covenants in place prohibiting certain work?'

Okay.

'What's your budget for kitting out your shop? See this shelving system here? It costs twice as much as that one. Is it worth twice as much to you? If it's not, which other shelving system do you settle on?'

'So…fitting the dream to the reality?'

'Exactly. Deciding on the nitty-gritty detail.'

He swung the computer back his way, his fingers flying across the keyboard, his brow furrowed in concentration and his lips pursed. As she stared at him something inside Audra's chest cracked open and she felt herself falling and falling and falling. Not 'scream and grab onto something' falling, but flying falling.

Like anything was possible falling.

Like falling in love falling.

Her heart stopped. The air in front of her eyes shimmered. Finn? She'd…she'd fallen in love with Finn? Her heart gave a giant kick and started beating in triple time. She swallowed. No, no, that was nonsense. She wasn't stupid enough to fall for Finn. He didn't do serious. He treated women as toys. He was a playboy!

And yet… He *did* do serious because they'd

had several very serious discussions while they'd been here. She'd discovered depths to him she'd never known. He wasn't just an adrenaline junkie, but a talented designer and canny businessman. The playboy thing… Well, he hadn't been out carousing every night. And he hadn't treated her like a toy. Even when she'd wanted him to. So it was more than possible that she had him pegged all wrong about that too.

In the next moment she shook her head. Rupert had warned her against Finn, and Rupert would know.

But…

She didn't want to kill the hope trickling through her. Was it really so stupid?

'Okay, here's a budget version of your shop.'

Finn turned the laptop back towards her. She forced herself to focus on his designs rather than the chaos of her mind. And immediately lost herself in the world he'd created.

'What do you think?'

'This is still beautiful.'

He grinned and her heart kicked against the walls of her chest. She brushed her fingers across the picture of the barrel of flowers standing by the front door. 'You have such a talent for this. Don't you miss it when you're off adventuring?'

Very slowly he reached across and closed the lid of his laptop. 'That's a "truth or dare" question, Audra. And the answer is yes.'

Her heart stuttered. So did her breath.

'I've been fighting it. Not wanting to acknowledge it.'

'Why not?'

'Because I want to be more than a boring, driven businessman.'

'That's not boring!' She pointed to his computer. 'That...it shows what an artist you are.'

Hooded eyes met hers. 'I lead this exciting life—living the dream. It should be enough.'

But she could see that it wasn't. 'Dreams can change,' she whispered.

He stared down at his hands. 'I've had a lot of time to think over the last fortnight...and our discussions have made me realise a few things.'

Her mouth went dry. In a part of her that she refused to acknowledge, she wanted him to tell her that he loved her and wanted to build a life and family with her. 'Like?' she whispered.

'Like how much the way I live my life has to do with my parents.'

'In what way?' She held her breath and waited to see if he would answer.

He shrugged, but she sensed the emotion beneath the casual gesture. 'I hated not having a home base when I was growing up. I hated the way we were constantly on the move. I hated that I didn't have any friends my own age. But when my parents died...' He dragged a hand down his face. 'I'd have done anything to have them back. But at the same time—' the breath he drew in was ragged '—I didn't want to give up the life Uncle Ned had created for me. I liked that life a hundred times better.'

Her heart squeezed at the darkness swirling in his eyes—the remembered grief and pain, the confusion and strange sense of relief. She understood how all those things could bewilder and baffle a person, making it impossible to see things clearly.

'And that made me feel guilty. So I've tried to mould my life on a balance between the kind of life they lived and the kind of life Ned lived. I wanted to make them all proud. Similar to the way you wanted to make your mother proud, I guess. I thought I could have the best of both worlds and be happy.'

'But you're not happy.'

He wanted it to be enough. She could see that. But the simple fact was it wasn't. And him wishing otherwise wouldn't change that fact.

She swallowed. 'Have you ever loved a song so much that you played it over and over and over, but eventually you play it too much and you wreck it somehow? And then you don't want to listen to it any more, and when you do unexpectedly hear it somewhere it doesn't give you the same thrill it once did?'

Hooded eyes lifted. 'I know what you mean.'

'Well, maybe that's what you've done with all of your adrenaline-junkie sports. Maybe you're all adrenalined out and now you need to find a new song that sings to your soul.'

He stared at her, scepticism alive in his eyes. 'This is more than that. This is the entire way I live my life. Walking away from it feels as if I'm criticising the choices my parents made.'

'I don't see it as a criticism. You're just…just forging your own path.'

He shrugged, but the darkness in his eyes belied the casual gesture. 'The thing is I can no longer hide from the fact that racing down a black ski run no longer gives me the thrill it once did, or that performing endless laps in a sports car is anything other than monotonous, and that trekking to base camp at Everest is just damned cold and uncomfortable.'

But she could see it left him feeling like a bad person—an ingrate.

He speared her with a glance. 'I can't hassle and lecture you about living your dreams and then hide from it when it applies to my own life. That'd make me a hypocrite on top of everything else.'

Her heart burned. She wanted to help him the way he'd helped her—give him the same clarity. 'How old was your father when he died?'

'Thirty-five.'

'So only a couple of years older than you are now?' She gave what she hoped was an expressive shrug. 'Who knows what he might've chosen to do if he'd lived longer?'

'Give up extreme sports, my father?' Finn snorted. 'You can't be serious.'

'Is it any crazier than me opening a shop?'

He smiled. 'That's not crazy. It's what you have a passion for. It's *exciting*.'

Her heart chugged with so much love she had to lower her gaze in case he saw it shining there. 'We can never know what the future might've held for your father, but he could've had a midlife crisis and decided to go back to Australia and…and start a hobby farm.'

A bark of laughter shot out of him.

'I know a lot of people have criticised the way your parents lived, wrote them off as irresponsible and frivolous.' And she guessed she was one of them. 'But they didn't hurt anyone living like they did; they paid their bills. They were...free spirits. And free spirits, Finn, would tell you to follow your heart and do the things that make you happy. And to not care what other people think.'

His head snapped up.

'If they were true free spirits they'd include themselves amongst those whose opinions didn't matter.'

She watched his mind race. 'What are you going to do?' she asked when she couldn't hold the question back any longer.

He shook his head. 'I've no idea.'

She swallowed. He needed time to work it out.

When his gaze returned to hers, though, it was full of warmth and...and something she couldn't quite define. Affection...laughter...wonder? 'It's been a hell of a holiday, Audra.'

Her name sounded like gold on his tongue. All she could do was nod.

A warm breeze ruffled her hair, loose tendrils tickling her cheek. She pulled it back into a tighter ponytail, trying to gather up all the loose strands. For some reason her actions made Finn smile. 'I'm going to get it cut,' she announced, not realising her intention until the words had left her.

His eyebrows shot up.

'Short. *Really* short. A pixie cut, perhaps. I hate it dangling about my face. I always have.'

'So how come you haven't cut it before now?'

She had no idea. 'Just stuck in the old ways of doing things, I guess. Walking a line I thought I should and presenting the image I thought I should, and not deviating from it. But now...'

'Now?'

'Now anything seems possible.' Even her and Finn didn't seem outside the realms of possibility. He cared for her, she knew that much. And look at everything they'd shared this last fortnight. Look how much he'd done for her. Look how much of an impact they'd had on each other. It had to mean something, right?

'I'm going to ask Anna in the village if she'll cut it for me.'

'When?'

'Maybe...maybe this afternoon.' If she could get an appointment.

He stared at her for a long moment and she had to fight the urge to fidget. 'What?'

'I did something.'

There was something in his tone—something uncertain, and a little defiant, and…a bit embarrassed, maybe? She didn't know what it meant. 'What did you do?'

He scratched a hand through his hair, his gaze skidding away. 'It might be best if I simply show you.'

'Okay. Now?'

He nodded.

'Where are we going? What's the dress code?'

'Into the village.' His gaze wandered over her and it left her burning and achy, prickly and full of need. 'And what you're wearing is just fine.'

They stopped at the hairdresser's first, because Finn insisted. When Anna said she could cut Audra's hair immediately Finn accepted the appointment on her behalf before she could say anything. Audra surveyed him, bemused and not a little curious.

'It'll give me some time to get set up properly,' he explained when he caught her stare.

She shook her head. 'I've no idea what you're talking about.'

'I know.' He leaned forward and pressed a kiss

to her brow. 'All will be revealed soon. I'll be back in an hour.'

He was gone before the fresh, heady scent of him had invaded her senses, before she could grab him by the collar of his shirt and kiss him properly. Dear God, what did she do with her feelings for him? She had no idea! Should she try to bury them...or did she dare hope that, given time, he could return them?

Don't do anything rash.

She swallowed and nodded. She couldn't afford to make another mistake. She and Thomas had only broken up six weeks ago. This could be a rebound thing. Except... She'd not been in love with Thomas. She'd wanted to be, but she could see now it'd been nothing but a pale imitation— a combination of loneliness and feeling flattered by his attentions. She pressed her hands to her stomach as it started to churn.

Don't forget Rupert warned you against falling in love with Finn.

Yeah, but Rupert was overprotective and—

'Audra, would you like to take a seat?'

Audra shook herself, and tried to quiet her mind as she gave herself over to Anna's ministrations.

*　*　*

As promised, Finn returned an hour later. Audra's hair had been cut, shampooed and blow-dried and it felt...*wonderful*! She loved what Anna had done—short at the back and sides but still thick and tousled on top. She ran her fingers through it, and the excitement she'd woken with this morning vibrated through her again now.

She and Anna were sharing a cup of tea and gossip when Finn returned, and the way his eyes widened when he saw her, the light that flared in his eyes, and the low whistle that left his lips, did the strangest things to her insides.

'It looks...' He gestured. 'I mean, you look...' He swallowed. 'It's great. You look great.'

Something inside her started to soar. He wanted her. He tried to hide it, but he wanted her in the same way she wanted him. It wasn't enough. But it was something, right? She could build on that, and... Her heart dipped. Except their holiday was almost over and there was so little time left—

He frowned. 'You're not regretting it, are you?'

She tried to clear her face. 'No! I love it.' She touched a self-conscious hand to her new do. 'It feels so liberating.' She did what she could to put her disturbing thoughts from her mind. 'Now put me out of my misery and show me whatever it is you've done. I'm dying here, Finn!'

'Come on, then.' He grinned and took her arm, but dropped it the moment they were outside. She knew why—because the pull between them was so intense.

What if she were to seduce him? Maybe…

That could be a really bad idea.

Or an inspired one.

Her heart picked up speed. She had to force herself to focus on where they were going.

Finn led her along the village's main street. She made herself glance into the windows of the fashion boutiques with their colourful displays, dragged in an appreciative breath as they passed the bakery that sold those decadent croissants. She slowed when they reached the bookshop, but with a low laugh Finn urged her past it.

At the end of the row stood the beautiful whitewashed building with freshly painted shutters the colour of a blue summer day that had silently sat at the centre of herÁ dreams. The moment she'd seen the For Sale sign when she'd clambered off the ferry a fortnight ago, she'd wanted to buy it. Her heart pounded. This place was…*perfect.*

'I remember you saying there was a place for

sale in the village that would be the ideal location for your shop, and I guessed this was the place you meant.'

She spun to him, her eyes wide.

'So I asked around and found it belongs to the Veros family.'

'The Veros family who own the deli?'

'One and the same. I asked if we could have a look inside.' He brandished a key. 'And they said yes.'

Excitement gathered beneath her breastbone until she thought she might burst.

'Shall we?'

'Yes, please!'

He unlocked the door. 'Do you want the shutters open?' He gestured to the shutters at the front window. She could barely speak so she simply nodded. She wanted to see the interior bathed in the blues and golds of the late morning light. 'You go on ahead, then, while I open them.'

Pressing one hand to her chest, she reached out with the other to push the door open. Her heart beat hard against her palm. Could this be the place where she could make her dreams come true? Was this the place where she could start the rest of her life? She tried to rein in her excitement. This was the next step—making the dream fit the reality. She needed to keep her feet on the ground.

Inside it was dim and shadowy. She closed her eyes and made a wish, and when she opened her eyes again, light burst through the spotlessly clear front window as Finn flung the shutters back. Her heart stuttered. The world tilted on its axis. She had to reach out and brace herself against a wall to stop from falling.

Her heart soared...stopped...pounded.

She couldn't make sense of what she was seeing, but in front of her the designs Finn had created for her shop had taken shape and form in this magical place. She squished her eyes shut, but when she opened them again nothing had changed.

She spun around to find Finn wrestling a tub of colourful flowers into place just outside the front door. Her eyes filled. He'd done all of this for her?

He came inside then and grinned, but she saw the uncertainty behind the smile. 'What do you think?'

'I think this is amazing! How on earth did you manage to do this in such a short space of time?'

One shoulder lifted. 'I asked Angelo to whip

up a couple of simple display arrangements—don't look too closely because they're not finished.'

'But…but there's stock on the shelves!'

'I borrowed some bits and pieces from Angelo, Eleni, Kostas and Christina. They were more than happy to help me out when I told them what it was for. You're very well thought of in these parts. They consider you one of their own, you know?'

It was how she'd always felt here.

'So you'll see it gets a little more rough and ready the further inside we go.'

He took her arm and led her deeper into the shop and she saw that he'd tacked pictures of all the things she meant to sell on temporary shelves. It brought her dream to magical life, however—helped her see how it could all look in reality. The layout and design, the colours and the light flooding in, the view of the harbour, it was all so very, *very* perfect. 'I love it.'

'Wait until you see upstairs.' Reaching for her hand, he towed her to the back of the shop. 'There's a kitchenette and bathroom through here and storeroom there.' He swung a door open and clicked on the light, barely giving her time to glance inside before leading her up a narrow set of stairs to a lovely apartment with a cosy living room, compact but adequate kitchen, and two bedrooms. The living room and the master bedroom, which was tucked beneath the eaves on the third floor, had exceptional views of the harbour. It was all *utterly* perfect.

'I can't believe you did this!'

'So you like it?'

'I couldn't love it any better.'

His grin was full of delight and…affection.

Her mind raced. He was attracted to her, and he cared for her. He'd done all of this for her. It had to *mean* something.

'I made enquiries and the price they're asking seems reasonable.'

He named a price that made her gulp, but was within her means. She pulled in a breath. 'I'm going to get a building inspection done and… and then put in an offer.'

He spun back to her. 'You mean it?'

She nodded. She wanted to throw herself at him and hug him. But if she did that it'd make his guard go back up. And before that happened she needed to work through the mass of confusion and turbulence racing through her mind.

She followed him back down the stairs silently.

His gaze narrowed when they reached the ground floor. 'Is everything okay?'

'My mind is racing at a hundred miles a minute. I'm feeling a little overwhelmed.'

His eyes gentled. 'That's understandable.'

She gestured around. 'Why did you do this for me, Finn? I'm not complaining. I love it. But…it must've taken a lot of effort on your part.'

'I just want you to have your dream, Princess. You deserve it.'

She stared at him, wishing she could read his mind. 'You've spent a lot of time thinking about my future, and I'm grateful. But don't you think you should've been spending that time focussing on some new directions for yourself?'

His gaze dropped. He straightened a nearby shelf, wiped dust from another. 'I've been giving some thought to that too.'

The admission made her blink. He had?

'Kyanós, it seems, encourages soul-searching.' He shoved his hands into the back pockets of his cargo shorts and eyed her for a long moment. 'I've been toying with a plan. I don't know. It could be a stupid idea.' He pulled his hands free, his fingers opening and closing at his sides. 'Do you want to see?'

Fear and hope warred in her chest. All she could do was nod.

'Come on, then. We'll return the key and then I'll show you.'

The car bounced along an unsealed road that was little more than a gravel track. Audra glanced at the forest of olive and pine trees that lined both sides. She'd thought he'd meant to take them back to the villa. 'I've not been on this road before.'

'I've spent some time exploring the island's hidden places these last few days.'

Along with exploring all the ways she could make her dream a reality. He'd been busy.

'It brings us out on the bluff at the other end of the beach from Rupert's place.'

The view when they emerged into a clearing five minutes later stole her breath. Finn parked and cut the engine. She pushed out of the car and just stared.

He shoved his hands into his pockets, keeping the car between them. 'It's a pretty amazing view.'

Understatement much? 'I'm not sure I've ever seen a more spectacular view. This is...*amazing*.' Water surrounded the headland on three sides.

From this height she could only make out a tiny strip of beach to her left and then Rupert's villa gleaming in amongst its pines in the distance.

Directly out in front was the Aegean reflecting the most glorious shade of blue that beguiled like a siren's call, the horizon tinted a fiery gold, the outlines of other islands in the distance adding depth and interest. It'd be a spectacular sight when the sun set.

To her right the land fell in gentle undulations, golden grasses rippling down to a small but perfectly formed beach. A third of the way down was a collection of run-down outbuildings.

'This plot—thirty acres in total—is for sale.' He pointed to the outbuildings. 'The farmer who owns it used those to store olives from his groves…and goats, among other things apparently. They haven't been used for almost fifteen years. The moment I clapped eyes on them I knew exactly how to go about transforming them into an amazing house.'

It was the perfect site for a home—sheltered and sunny, and with that beautiful view. Audra swallowed. 'That sounds lovely.'

'I even came up with a name for the house—the Villa Óneira.'

Óneira was the Greek word for dreams. The

House of Dreams. He…he wanted to live here on Kyanós? Her heart leapt. *That* had to mean something.

She tried to keep her voice casual. 'What would you do with the rest of the plot?' Because no matter how hard she tried, she couldn't see Finn as an olive farmer or a goat herder.

He gestured to the crest of the headland. 'Do you remember once asking me what activities I couldn't live without?'

She'd been thinking of the rally-car racing, the rock climbing, the skydiving. 'What's the answer?'

'Hang-gliding.'

She blinked. 'Hang-gliding?'

'It's the best feeling in the world. Sailing above it all on air currents—weightless, free… exhilarating.'

Her heart burned as she stared at him. He looked so *alive*.

'That was a great question to ask, Audra, because it made me think hard about my life.'

It had?

'And when I stumbled upon this plot of land and saw that headland, I knew what I could do here.'

She found it suddenly hard to breathe.

'I've been fighting it and telling myself it's a stupid pipe dream.' He swung to her, his face more animated than she'd ever seen it. 'But after our talk this morning, maybe it's not so daft after all.'

'What do you want to do?'

'I want to open a hang-gliding school. I'm a fully qualified instructor.'

He was?

'And I've had a lot of experience.'

He had?

'The school would only run in the summer.' He shrugged. 'For the rest of the time I'd like to focus on the work I do for Aspiration Designs. But I want to work off the grid.' He flung out an arm. 'And here seems as good a place to do it as any. Kyanós has a great community vibe, and I'd love to become a part of it.'

He stopped then as if embarrassed, shoved his hands in his pockets and scuffed a tussock of grass with the toe of his sneaker.

She stared at him. His dream... It was lovely. Beautiful. 'Your plan sounds glorious, Finn.'

He glanced up. 'But?'

She shook her head. 'No buts. It's just... I remember you saying island life wouldn't suit you.'

'I was wrong. Being on a permanent holiday

wouldn't suit me. But being in an office all day wouldn't suit me either. I'd want to leave the day-to-day running of Aspirations to my partners—they're better at that than me. Design is my forte. But the thought of sharing my love of hang-gliding with others and teaching them how to do it safely in this amazing place answers a different need.'

'Wow.' She couldn't contain a grin. 'Looks like we're going to be neighbours.'

He grinned back and it nearly dazzled her. 'Looks like it. Who'd have thought?'

This had to mean something—something big! Even if he wasn't aware of it yet.

He tossed the car keys in the air and caught them. 'Hungry?'

'Starved.'

CHAPTER ELEVEN

'LOOKS LIKE YOUR sailboat is coming in again, Audra.'

They were eating a late lunch of crusty bread, cheese and olives, and Audra's mind was buzzing with Finn's plans for the future. If they were both going to be living on Kyanós, then...

Her heart pounded. It was possible that things could happen. Romantic things. She knew he hadn't considered settling down, falling in love—marrying and babies. Not yet. But who knew how that might change once he settled into a new life here? Given time, who knew what he might choose to do?

She tried to control the racing of her pulse. She had no intention of rushing him. *She* was in no rush. She meant to enjoy their friendship, and to relish the changes she was making in her life. And—she swallowed—they would wait and see what happened.

He'd risen to survey the beach below. She moved to stand beside him, and was greeted with the now familiar pink and blue sail. 'It looks like they're coming ashore.'

Heat burned her cheeks when she recalled her earlier musings about the honeymooners who might be on board. She hoped they weren't planning to have hot sex on her beach. Not that it was *hers* per se, but... She turned her back on the view, careful not to look at Finn. 'Do you want any more of these olives or cheese?'

He swung back and planted himself at the table again. 'Don't take the olives! They're the best I've ever eaten.'

She tried to laugh, rather than sigh, at the way he savoured one.

He helped himself to another slice of a Greek hard cheese called *kefalotiri*. 'Whose turn is it to choose the activities for the day?'

She helped herself to a tiny bunch of grapes. 'I've no idea.' She'd lost count. Besides, the day was half over.

'Then I vote that a long lazy lunch is the order of the day.'

She laughed for real this time. 'It's already been long and lazy.'

'We could make it longer and lazier.'

Sounded good to her.

'We could open a bottle of wine…grab our books…'

Okay, it sounded perfect. 'Count me in.'

'We could head down to the beach if you want…'

She shook her head. 'Let the visitors enjoy it in privacy. I'm stuffed too full of good food to swim.'

He grinned. 'I'll grab the wine.'

'I'll grab our books.'

But before either of them could move, the sound of voices and crackling undergrowth had them looking towards the track. Audra blinked when Rupert, accompanied by a woman she didn't know, emerged.

A smile swept through her—he should've let them know he was coming! Before she could leap up, however, Finn's low, savage curse had her senses immediately going on high alert. She glanced at him, and her stomach nosedived at the expression on his face.

Finn rose.

Rupert and the woman halted when they saw him. The air grew thick with a tension Audra didn't understand. Nobody spoke.

She forced herself to stand too. 'What's going on, Finn?'

He glanced down at her and she recognised regret and guilt swirling in his eyes, and something else she couldn't decipher. 'I really should've told you about that woman in Nice I'd been trying to avoid. I'm sorry, Princess.'

Audra stared at the woman standing beside Rupert—a tall, leggy brunette whose eyes were hidden behind a large pair of sunglasses—and her mouth went dry. That gorgeous woman was Finn's latest girlfriend? Her stomach shrivelled to the size of a small hard pebble. *Why* had Rupert brought her to the island? She recalled his warnings about Finn and closed her eyes.

'Trust me!'

Her eyes flew open at Finn's words. She wasn't sure if they were a command or a plea.

His eyes burned into hers. 'I promise I will not allow anything she does to hurt you.'

What on earth…?

'You're going to make damn sure of it,' Rupert snarled, striding forwards. He kissed her cheek with a clipped, 'Squirt.' But the glare he shot Finn filled her stomach with foreboding. And it turned Finn grey. 'Audra, this is Trixie McGraw.'

The woman held out her hand. Audra shook it. Trixie? She *hated* that name. It took all her strength to stop her lips from twisting.

'What Rupert has left out of his introduction,' Finn drawled, 'is that Ms McGraw here is an investigative journalist. *Not* an ex-girlfriend, *not* an ex-lover.'

She wasn't...

She was a journalist!

Audra swung to Rupert, aghast. 'You've brought the press to the island?'

Rupert opened his mouth, but Finn cut in. 'She's not here for you, Audra. She wants to interview me.'

'Why?'

If possible, Finn turned even greyer and she wanted to take his hand and offer him whatever silent support she could, but Rupert watched them both with such intensity she didn't want to do anything he could misinterpret. She didn't want to do anything that would damage their friendship.

'My recent accident—the ski-jump disaster—it happened on a resort owned by a friend, Joachim Firrelli. Trixie here was Joachim's girlfriend before they had an ugly bust-up. She's now trying to prove that his facilities are substandard—that he's to blame for my accident. Except I'm not interested in being a pawn in her little game of revenge.'

'It doesn't sound *little* to me. It sounds bitter and a lot twisted.'

Trixie didn't bat so much as an eyelid. Rupert's mouth tightened.

'As I've repeatedly told Ms McGraw, the accident was nobody's fault but my own. I lost concentration. End of story. And I'm not going to let a friend of mine pay the price for my own recklessness.'

His guilt made sudden and sickening sense. He felt guilty that his actions could cause trouble for his friend. And he felt guilty that he'd unwittingly attracted a member of the press to the island when she was doing all that she could to avoid them. *Oh, Finn.*

Finn had crossed his arms and his mouth was set. Her heart pounded, torn between two competing impulses. One was the nausea-inducing reminder that Finn wasn't the kind of man to settle down with just one woman and that to love him would leave her with nothing but a broken heart.

The other…well, it continued to hope. After all, he'd wasted no time in telling her who this Trixie McGraw was, and what she wanted from him. He hadn't wanted her to think this woman was a girlfriend or lover, and that had to mean something, right?

She glared at Rupert. 'Why on earth...? Did you *know* this woman was on a witch hunt?'

Rupert's hands fisted. He turned to Trixie. 'Is what Finn said true?'

One shoulder lifted. 'Pretty much. Except for the "witch hunt" part.'

The woman had the most beautiful speaking voice Audra had ever heard.

'Your sister seems to think I'm motivated by revenge, though I can assure you that is not the case. I believe it's in the public interest to know when the safety standards on a prominent ski resort have deteriorated.'

It was all Audra could do not to snort. 'I can't believe you've brought the media to the island.' Not when he'd done everything he could to protect her from the attention of the press before she'd arrived here.

'I didn't *bring* her. She was already here. I received an email from her yesterday. That's why I'm here now. I left Geneva this morning. I'm not this woman's friend.'

She took a moment to digest that.

So... None of them wanted to talk to this woman?

The press had made her life hell back in Geneva. She wasn't going to let that happen again here on the island. She wasn't going to let them turn Finn and his friend Joachim into their next victims either. She folded her arms. 'Rupert, you have a choice to make.'

He blinked. 'What choice?'

She met his gaze. It was sombre and focussed. 'This is your house. You can invite whomever you want. But you either choose me or you choose her, because one of us has to leave. And if you do choose her, there will be repercussions. There won't be any family dinners in the foreseeable future, and you can kiss a family Christmas goodbye.'

Rupert's nostrils flared.

'Audra,' Finn started, but she waved him quiet.

'I don't trust her, Rupe, but I do trust Finn.' Something in Rupert's eyes darkened and it made her blink. *Wow.* He didn't? When had that happened? She swallowed. 'And you trust me, so—'

'Forgive me, Ms Russel,' the beautiful voice inserted. 'I understand your current aversion to the press given the circus surrounding your relationship with Thomas Farquhar but I'm not here to discuss that. Your privacy is assured.'

Maybe, but Finn's wasn't. She ignored her. 'I want her off this property. Choose, Rupert.'

'It's no competition, Squirt. You'd win in a heartbeat. But I need your help with something first. We won't go inside the house, I promise. But bear with me here. This will take ten minutes. Less. If you still want Trixie to leave after that, I'll escort her off the premises.'

It didn't seem too much to ask. And in the face of Rupert's sheer reasonableness she found her outrage diminishing. 'Ten minutes.' She pulled out her phone and set a timer.

Rupert motioned to Trixie and she pulled a large A4 manila envelope from her backpack and placed it on the table. Rupert gestured for her and Finn to take a look at the contents. His glance, when it clashed with Finn's, was full of barely contained violence that made Finn's gaze narrow and his shoulders stiffen. Wasting no further time, she reached inside the envelope and pulled out…photographs.

She inhaled sharply, and her heart plummeted. Pictures of her and Finn.

The first captured the moment yesterday when she'd leant forward and in the excitement of the moment had kissed Finn. The next showed the moment after when they'd stared at each other—

yearning and heat palpable in both their faces. She could feel the heat of need rising through her again now. She flipped to the next one. It was of her and Finn drinking champagne in a harbourside tavern afterwards. They were both smiling and laughing. And she couldn't help it, her lips curved upwards again now. This dreadful woman had captured one of the happiest moments of Audra's life.

'This is what you do?' she asked the other woman. 'You spy on people?'

Trixie, probably wisely, remained silent.

She glanced at Rupert. 'You're upset about this? I know you warned Finn off, but *I* kissed *him*, not the other way around. I took him off guard. He didn't stand a chance.' Behind her Finn snorted. 'Besides, it was a friendly kiss... a thank-you kiss. And it lasted for less than two seconds.'

Without a word, Rupert leaned across and pulled that photo away to reveal the one beneath. She stared at it and everything inside her clenched up tight. It was of her and Finn outside the art studio that day, and they were... She fought the urge to fan her face. They were oblivious to everything. They were wrapped so tightly in each other's arms it was impossible to tell where one began and the other ended. It had, quite simply, been the best kiss of her life.

She lifted her head and shrugged. 'I'm not sure she got my best side.'

Nobody laughed.

'Trixie has informed me that unless she gets an interview with Finn, she'll sell these photos to the tabloids.' Rupert speared Finn with a glare that made all the hairs on her arms lift. 'Finn *will* give her that interview and make sure *you* aren't subjected to any more grubby media attention.'

A fortnight ago she might've agreed with Rupert, but now... She drew in a breath, then lifted her chin. 'I'm not ashamed of these photos.'

'It's okay, Princess. I don't mind. I don't have anything incriminating to tell our fair crusader here, so an interview won't take long at all.'

She wanted to stamp her feet in her sudden frustration. 'No, you're not hearing me. *I'm not ashamed of these photographs.*'

He met her gaze, stilled, and then rocked back on his heels. 'I—'

She held up a hand and shook her head. Pursing his lips, he stared at her for what seemed like forever, and then eventually nodded, and she knew he was allowing her to choose how they'd progress from here. She swung back to Rupert and Trixie. 'In fact, I'm so *not* ashamed of these photographs, if Ms McGraw doesn't mind, I'm going to keep them.'

'I have the digital files saved in several different locations. Your keeping that set won't prevent them from being made public.'

'I didn't doubt that for a moment.' Audra's phone buzzed. 'Time's up, Rupert.'

'You still want her to leave?'

'Absolutely! I'd much rather these pictures appear in the papers than any more gratuitous speculation about me and Thomas.' The situation with Thomas had left her feeling like a fool, not to mention helpless and a victim. The pictures of her and Finn, however… Well, they didn't.

'Besides, we all know how the press can twist innocent words to suit their own purposes. It sounds to me as if Joachim doesn't deserve to become the next target in a media scandal that has no substance.'

'You're mistaken. There's substance,' Trixie said.

'Then go find your evidence elsewhere, because you're not going to hit the jackpot here,' Audra shot back.

Rupert's eyes flashed as he turned to Finn. 'So you refuse to do the honourable thing?'

* * *

Rupert's words felt like a knife to his chest. Finn refused to let his head drop. 'I'm going to do whatever Audra wants us to do.' He'd known how disempowered Farquhar had left her feeling. He wasn't going to let Trixie McGraw make her feel the exact same way. *He* wasn't going to make her feel that same way.

He'd sensed that the photographs had both amused and empowered her, though he wasn't sure why. She'd been amazing to watch as she'd dealt with the situation—strong and capable, invulnerable. He wasn't raining on her parade now.

Rupert's hands clenched. 'You promised you wouldn't mess with her!'

Finn braced himself for the impact of Rupert's fist against his jaw, but Audra inserted herself between them. 'Not in front of Lois Lane here, please, Rupe.' She pointed back down the path. 'I believe you mentioned something about escorting her from the premises.'

A muscle in Rupert's jaw worked. 'You sure about this?'

'Positive.'

Trixie shook her head. 'You're making a mistake.'

'And you're scum,' Audra shot back.

Amazingly, Trixie laughed. As Rupert led her to the top of the path, she said, 'I like your sister.'

'I'm afraid she doesn't return the favour. I'll meet you back on the boat later.'

Without another word, Trixie started back down to the beach. She waved to them all when she reached the bottom.

'I think we should take this inside,' Audra said, when Rupert turned to stare at Finn.

Finn's heart slugged like a sick thing in his chest. He'd kissed Audra, and Rupert's sense of betrayal speared into him in a thousand points of pain.

Rupert hadn't been joking when he'd said he'd no longer consider Finn a friend if Finn messed about with Audra. Finn had to brace his hands against his knees at the sense of loss that pounded through him. He'd destroyed the most important friendship of his life. This was his fault, no one else's. The blame was all his. He forced himself to straighten. 'I think we'll do less damage out here, Audra.'

'The two of you are *not* fighting.'

He met the other man's gaze head-on. 'I'm not going to fight, Princess.' But if Rupert wanted to pound him into the middle of next week, he'd let him. Rupert's eyes narrowed and Finn saw that he'd taken his meaning.

'*Rupe,*' Audra warned.

Rupert made for the house. 'You're not worth the bruised knuckles.'

The barb hit every dark place in Finn's soul. He'd never been worth the sacrifice Rupert had made for him. He'd never been worth the sacrifices he'd always wanted his parents to make for him.

Hell! A fortnight on this island with Audra and he'd laid his soul bare. He lifted his arms and let them drop. He didn't know what any of it meant. What he did know was that this Greek island idyll was well and truly over. He wanted to roar and rage at that, but he had no right.

No right at all. So he followed Rupert and Audra into the house, and it was all he could do to walk upright rather than crawl.

They went into the living room. Audra glanced from Rupert to Finn and back again. 'I think we need to talk about that kiss.'

Finn fell into an armchair. Was it too early for a whisky? 'It won't help.' He'd broken his word and that was that. He'd blown it.

Rupert settled on the sofa, stretched his legs

out. 'I'm interested in what you have to say, Squirt.' He ignored Finn.

'The kiss—the steamy one—it wasn't calculated, you know?'

She twisted her hands together and more than anything Finn wanted to take them and kiss every finger. He hated the thought of anything he'd done causing her distress. *You should've thought about that before kissing her!*

For a moment he felt the weight of Rupert's stare, but he didn't meet it. The thought of confronting the other man's disgust left him exhausted.

'It was Finn who ended the kiss. I wanted to take it to its natural conclusion, but Finn held back because of how much he feels he owes you.'

He sensed the subtle shift in Rupert's posture. 'You know about that?'

She nodded. 'I'm glad you did what you did when you were sixteen, Rupe. It was a good thing to do.' She folded her arms. 'But it doesn't change the fact that I'm furious with you at the moment.'

Rupert stiffened. 'With me?'

She leaned forward and poked a finger at him. 'You have no right to interfere in my love life.

I can kiss whoever I want, and you don't get to have any say in that.'

Finn dragged a hand down his face, trying to stop her words from burrowing in beneath his flesh. Rupert knew Finn wasn't good enough for his sister. Finn knew it too.

'I understand the kiss,' Rupert growled. 'I get the spur-of-the-moment nature of being overwhelmed before coming to your senses. I understand attraction and desire. None of those things worry me, Squirt.' He reached for the photos she'd set on the coffee table, rifled through them and then held one up. '*This* is what worries me.'

Audra stilled, and then glanced away, rubbing a hand across her chest.

Finn glanced at it. What the hell…? It was the second photo—the one after the kiss. Okay, there was some heat in the way they looked at each other, but that picture was innocent. 'What the hell is wrong with that?'

Rupert threw him a withering glare before turning his attention back to his sister. 'Have you fallen in love with him?'

Every cell in Finn's body stiffened. His breathing grew ragged and uneven. What the hell was Rupert talking about?

'Princess?' He barely recognised the croak that was his voice.

Her face fell as if something inside her had crumbled. 'Your timing sucks, big brother.'

'You're family. You matter to me. I don't want to see you hurt. Have you fallen in love with Finn?'

Her chin lifted and her eyes sparked. 'Yes, I have. What's more I don't regret it. I think you're wrong about him.'

Finn shot to his feet. 'You can't have! That's not possible!' He pointed a finger at her. 'We talked about this.'

Audra's chin remained defiant. 'We talked about a lot of things.'

They had and—

He shook himself. 'None of what I said means I'm ready to settle down.'

Her hands went to her hips, but the shadows in her eyes made his throat burn. 'I think that's *exactly* what it means. I just think you're too afraid to admit it to yourself.'

He might be ready to put his freewheeling, adrenaline-loving days behind him, but it didn't mean he'd ever be ready for a white picket fence.

Even as he thought it, though, a deep yearning welled inside him.

He ignored it. Happy families weren't for him. They hadn't worked out when he was a child and he had no faith they'd work out for him as a man. 'Look, Audra, what you're feeling at the moment is just a by-product of your excitement... for all the changes you're going to make in your life, and—'

From the corner of his eyes he saw Rupert lean forward.

'And the romance of the Greek islands.' If he called her Squirt now, she'd tell him that was Strike Three and...and it'd all be over. He opened his mouth, but the word refused to come.

Audra drew herself up to her full height, her eyes snapping blue fire. 'Don't you dare presume to tell me what I'm feeling. I know exactly what I'm feeling. *I love you, Finn.*' She dragged in a shaky breath. 'And I know this feels too soon for you to admit, but you either love me too. Or you don't. But I'm not letting you off the hook with platitudes like that.'

He flinched.

Her eyes filled and he hated himself. He glanced at Rupert. The other man stared back, his gaze inscrutable. Finn wished he'd shoot off that sofa and beat him to a pulp. Rupert turned back to Audra. 'When did he start calling you Princess?'

He could see her mentally go back over their previous conversations. 'After that kiss—the steamy one.'

Rupert pursed his lips. 'He doesn't do endearments. He never has.'

What the hell…? That didn't mean anything!

Audra moved a step closer then as if Rupert's observation had given her heart. 'You might want to look a little more closely, a little more deeply, at the reasons it's been so important to you to look after me this last fortnight.'

'I haven't looked after you!' He didn't do nurturing.

'What do you call it, then?' She started counting things off on her fingers. 'You've fed me up. You forced me to exercise. And you made sure I got plenty of sun and R & R.'

He rolled his shoulders. 'You were too skinny.' And she'd needed to get moving—stop moping. Exercise was a proven mood enhancer. As for the sun and the R & R… 'We're on a Greek island!' He lifted his hands. 'When in Rome…'

Her eyes narrowed. 'You read a book on the beach, Finn. If that's not going above and beyond…'

Rupert's head snapped up. 'He read a book? *Finn* read a book?' Audra glared at him and he held his hands out. 'Sorry, staying quiet again now.'

So what? He'd read a book. He'd *liked* the book.

'And that's before we get to the really important stuff like you challenging me to follow a path that will make me happy—truly happy.' She swallowed. 'And don't you think it's revealing that you sensed that dream when no one else ever has?'

His mouth went dry. 'That's...that's just because of how much time we've been spending together recently—a by-product of forced proximity.'

She snorted. 'There was nothing forced about it. We spent three days avoiding each other, Finn. We never had to spend as much time together as we did.' She folded her arms and held his gaze. 'And I know you spent those three days thinking about me.'

His head reared back.

'You spent that time bringing my dream to full Technicolor life.'

He scowled. 'Nonsense. I just showed you what

it could look like.' He'd wanted to convince her she could do it.

'And while you're analysing your motives for why you did all those things for me, you might also want to consider why it is you've enjoyed being looked after by me so much too.'

She hadn't—

He stared at her. 'That ridiculous nonsense of yours when we went running… And then making sure I didn't overdo it when we went jetskiing.' Enticing him to read not just a book, but a trilogy that had hooked him totally. 'You wanted me to take it easy after my accident.'

She'd been clever and fun, and she'd made him laugh. He hadn't realised what she'd been up to. She'd challenged him in ways that had kept his mind, not just active, but doing loop-the-loops, while his body had been recuperating and recovering its strength. *Clever.*

'You haven't chafed the slightest little bit at the slower pace.'

Because it hadn't felt slow. It'd felt perfect. Everything inside him stilled. *Perfect?* Being here with Audra…? She made him feel… He swallowed. She made him feel as if he were hanggliding.

She was perfect.

Things inside him clenched up. She said that she loved him.

'You're planning to move to the island too. Don't you think that means something?'

It felt as if a giant fist had punched him in the stomach. He saw now exactly what it did mean. He loved her. He wasn't sure at what point in the last fortnight that'd happened, but it had. *She said she loved him.* His heart pounded. With everything he had he wanted to reach out and take it, but...

He glanced at Rupert. Rupert stared back, his dark eyes inscrutable, and a cold, dank truth swamped Finn in darkness. Acid burned hot in his gut. Rupert *knew* Finn wasn't good enough for his sister. Rupert knew Finn couldn't make Audra happy...he knew Finn would let her down.

A dull roar sounded in his ears; a throbbing pounded at his temples.

'I have a "truth or dare" question for you, Finn.'

He forced himself to meet her gaze.

'Do you or don't you love me?'

The question should've made him flinch, but it didn't. He loved her more than life itself. And if he denied it, he knew exactly how much pain that'd inflict on her. He knew exactly how it'd devastate her.

He glanced at Rupert. He glanced back at her. She filled his vision. He'd helped her find her dream, had helped her find the courage to pursue it. That was no small thing. She would lead a happier life because of it. And he—

He swung to Rupert, his hands forming fists. 'Look, I know you don't think I'm good enough for your little sister, and you're probably right! But you don't know how amazing she is. If I have to fight you over this I will, but—'

Rupert launched himself out of his seat. 'What the hell! I *never* said you weren't good enough for Audra. When have I ever given you the impression that you weren't good enough?'

Finn's mouth opened and closed, but no sound came out.

'When have I ever belittled you, made light of your achievements, or treated you like you weren't my equal?'

Rupert's fists lifted and Finn kept a careful eye on them, ready to dodge if the need arose. He'd rarely seen Rupert so riled.

'That's just garbage!' Rupert slashed a hand through the air. 'Garbage talk from your own mind, because you still feel so damn guilty about me giving up that stupid prize all those years ago.'

Rupert glared at him, daring him to deny it. Finn's mind whirled. He'd carried the guilt of what Rupe had sacrificed for him for seventeen years. He'd used that guilt to keep him on the straight and narrow, but in the process had it skewed his thinking?

'But you ordered me to keep my distance from Audra. *Why?*'

'Because I always sensed you could break her heart. And with you so hell-bent on avoiding commitment I—'

'Because of the promise he made to himself when he was eighteen,' Audra inserted.

'What promise?' Rupert stared from one to the other. He shook himself. 'It doesn't matter. The thing is, I never realised Audra had the potential to break your heart too.'

Finn couldn't say anything. He could feel the weight of Audra's stare, but he wasn't ready to turn and meet it. 'You saved my life, Rupe.' Rupert went to wave it away, but Finn held a hand up to forestall him. 'But Audra is the one who's made me realise I need to live that life properly.'

Rupert dragged a hand down his face. 'I should never have interfered. It wasn't fair. I should've kept my nose well and truly out, and I hope the two of you can forgive me.' He looked at Audra. 'You're right to be furious with me. It's just…'

'You've got used to looking out for me. I know that. But, Rupe, I've got this.'

He nodded. 'I'm going to make myself scarce.'

She nodded. 'That would be appreciated.'

He leaned forward to kiss the top of her head. 'I love you, Squirt.' And then he reached forward and clapped Finn on the shoulder. 'I'll be back tomorrow.' And then he was gone.

Finn turned towards Audra. She stared at him, her eyes huge in her face. 'You haven't answered my question yet,' she whispered.

He nodded. 'All my life I've thought I've not been worthy of family…or commitment. I never once thought I was worth the sacrifice Rupert made for me seventeen years ago.'

'Finn.'

She moved towards him, but he held up a hand. 'I can see now that my parents left me with a hell of a chip on my shoulder, and a mountain-sized inferiority complex. All of my racing around choosing one extreme sport after another was just a way to try to feel good about myself.'

She nodded.

'It even worked for a while. Until I started wanting more.'

Her gaze held his. 'How much more?'

He moved across to cup her face. 'Princess, you've made me realise that I can have it *all*.'

A tear slipped down her cheek. She sent him a watery smile. 'Of course you can.'

A smile built through him. 'I want the whole dream, Audra. Here on Kyanós with you.'

Her chin wobbled. 'The whole dream?'

She gasped when he went down on one knee in front of her. 'At the heart of all this is you, Princess. It's you and your love that makes me complete. I love you.' He willed her to believe every word, willed her to feel how intensely he meant them. 'I didn't know I could ever love anyone the way I love you. The rest of it doesn't matter. If you hate the idea of me opening up a hang-gliding school I'll do something different. If you'd prefer to live in the village rather than on the plot of land I'm going to buy, then that's fine with me too. I'll make any sacrifice necessary to make you happy.'

Her eyes shimmered and he could feel his throat thicken.

He took her hands in his and kissed them. 'I'm sorry it took me so long to work it out. But I realise now that I'm not my father…and I'm not my mother. I'm in charge of my own life, and I mean to make it a good life. And it's a life I want to share with you, if you'll let me.'

Tears spilled down her cheeks.

'Audra Russel, will you do me the very great honour of marrying me and becoming my wife?'

And then he held his breath and waited. She'd said she loved him. But had he just screwed up here? Had he rushed her before she was ready? Had—?

She dropped to her knees in front of him, took his face in her hands and pulled his head down to hers. Heat and hunger swept through him at the first contact, spreading like an inferno until he found himself sprawled on the floor with her, both of them straining to get closer and closer to each other. Eventually she pulled back, pushed upwards and rolled until she straddled him. 'That was a yes, by the way.' She traced her fingers across his broad chest. 'I love your dream, Finn. I love you.'

He stroked her cheek, his heart filled with warmth and wonder. 'I don't know how I got so lucky. I'm going to make sure you never regret this decision. I'm going to spend the rest of my life making you happy.'

She bit her lip. 'Can…can you take me back to your plot of land?'

'What, now?' Right this minute?

She nodded, but looked as if she was afraid he'd say no.

He pulled his baser instincts back into line and hauled them both upright. Without another word, he moved her in the direction of the car. From now on he had every intention of making her every wish come true.

Audra stared at the amazing view and then at the man who stood beside her. She pointed towards the little bay. 'Do you think we could have a jetski?'

'Will that make you happy?'

'Yes.'

'Then we can have two.'

She turned and wrapped her arms around his neck. He pulled her in close; the possessiveness of the gesture and the way his eyes darkened thrilled her to the soles of her feet. 'I want you to teach me to hang-glide.'

His eyes widened. Very slowly he nodded. 'I can do that.'

She stared deep into his eyes and all the love she felt for him welled inside her. She felt euphoric that she no longer had to hide it. 'Do you know why I wanted to come here this afternoon?'

'Why?'

'Because I want *this* to be the place where we start our life together.' She swallowed. 'I love your vision of our future. And this…'

He raised an eyebrow. 'This…?'

She raised an eyebrow too and he laughed. 'Spot on,' he told her. 'The practice has paid off.'

Heat streaked through her cheeks then. His eyebrow lifted a little higher. 'Is that a blush, Princess?' His grin was as warm as a summer breeze. 'I'm intrigued.'

Suddenly embarrassed, she tried to ease away from him, but his hands trailed down her back to her hips, moulding her to him and making her gasp and ache and move against him restlessly instead. 'Tell me what you want, Audra.'

'You,' she whispered, meeting his gaze. He was right. There was no need for secrets or coyness or awkwardness. Not now. She loved him. And the fact that he loved her gave her wings. 'I wanted to come here because this is where I want our first time to be.' She lifted her chin. 'And I want that first time to happen this afternoon.'

His eyes darkened even further. His nostrils

flared, and he lifted a hand to toy with a button on her blouse, a question in his eyes.

She shook her head, her breath coming a little too fast. 'No more kisses out in the open, thank you very much. I bet Lois Lane is still lurking around here somewhere. And one set of photographs in circulation is more than enough.'

He laughed.

She glanced down the hill at the outbuildings. 'Why don't you walk me through your plans for our home?'

He grinned a slow grin that sent her pulse skyrocketing, before sliding an arm about her waist and drawing her close as they walked down the slope. 'What an excellent plan. I hope you don't have anywhere you need to be for the next few hours, Princess. My plans are...big.' He waggled his eyebrows. 'And it'd be remiss of me to not show them to you in comprehensive detail.'

'That,' she agreed, barely able to contain her laughter and her joy, 'would be *very* remiss of you.'

When they reached the threshold of what looked as if it were once a barn, he swung her up into his arms. 'Welcome home, Princess.'

She wrapped her arms about his neck. *He* was

her home. Gazing into his eyes, she whispered, 'It's a beautiful home, Finn. The best. I love it.'

His head blocked out the setting sun as it descended towards her, and she welcomed his kiss with everything inside her as they both started living the rest of their lives *right now.*

EPILOGUE

'Go! Go, *PAIDI MOU*!'

Audra laughed as Maria shooed her in the direction of Finn, who was waiting beside a nearby barrel of flowers in full bloom. The town square was still full of happy holidaymakers and *very* satisfied vendors.

'You listen to my wife, Audra,' Angelo said with a wide grin. 'Your husband wants to spend some time with his beautiful wife. Go and drink some wine and eat some olives, and bask in the satisfaction of what you've achieved over the last three days.'

'What *we've* achieved,' she corrected. 'And there's still things to—'

'We have it under control,' Maria told her with a firm nod. 'You work too hard. Go play now.'

Audra submitted with a laugh, and affectionate pecks to the cheeks of the older couple who'd become so very dear to both her and Finn during the last fourteen months since they'd moved to the island.

As if afraid she'd change her mind and head back to work, Finn sauntered across to take her hand. As always, it sent a thrill racing through her. *Her husband.* A sigh of pure appreciation rose through her.

'You make her put her feet up, Finn,' Maria ordered.

He saluted the older woman, and, sliding an arm around Audra's shoulders, led her down towards the harbour. Audra slipped her arm around his waist, leaning against him and relishing his strength. They'd been married for eight whole months, but she still had to pinch herself every day.

Standing on tiptoe, she kissed him. 'I think we can safely say the festival went well.'

'It didn't just *go well*, Princess.' He grinned down at her. 'It's been a resounding success. The festival committee has pulled off the event of the year.'

She stuck her nose in the air. 'The event of the year was our wedding, thank you very much.' They'd been married here on the island in the tiny church, and it had been perfect.

His grin widened. 'Okay, it was the second biggest event of the year. And there are plans afoot for next year already.'

He found a vacant table at Thea Laskari's harbourside taverna. 'I promised Thea you'd be across for her *kataifi*.'

They'd no sooner sat than a plate of the sweet nutty pastry was placed in front of them, along with a carafe of sparkling water. 'Yum!' She'd become addicted to these in recent weeks.

'On the house,' Ami, the waitress, said with a smile. 'Thea insists. If we weren't so busy she'd be out here herself telling everyone how fabulous the festival has been for business.' Ami glanced around the crowded seating area with a grin. 'I think we can safely predict that the festival cheer will continue well into the night. Thea sends her love and her gratitude.'

'And give her mine,' Audra said.

She did a happy dance when Ami left to wait on another table. 'Everyone has worked so hard. And it's all paid off.' She gestured at the main street and the town square, all festooned in gaily coloured bunting and stall upon stall of wares and produce. Satisfaction rolled through her. It'd been a lot of work and it'd taken a lot of vision, but they'd created something here they could all be proud of.

'*You've* worked so hard.' Finn lifted her hand

to his mouth and kissed it, and just like that the blood heated up in her veins.

'I heard Giorgos tell Spiros that next year the committee needs to market Kyanós as an authentic Greek getaway. With so many of the young people leaving the island, most families have a spare room they can rent out—so people can come here to get a bona fide taste of genuine Greek island life.'

She laughed. 'Everyone has been so enthusiastic.'

'This is all your doing, you know?'

'Nonsense!'

'You were the one that suggested the idea and had everyone rallying behind it. You've been the driving force.'

'*Everyone* has worked hard.'

He stared at her for a long moment. 'You're amazing, you know that? I don't know how I got to be so lucky. I love you, Audra Sullivan.'

Her throat thickened at the love in his eyes. She blinked hard. 'And I love you, Finn Sullivan.' This was the perfect time to tell him her news—with the sun setting behind them, and the air warm and fragrant with the scent of jasmine.

She opened her mouth but he spoke first. 'I had a word with Rupert earlier.'

She could tell from the careful way he spoke that Rupert had told him the outcome of the court case against Thomas Farquhar. She nodded. 'I had a quiet word with Trixie.'

Finn shook his head. 'I can't believe you're becoming best friends with a reporter.'

'I believe it might be Rupert who's her best friend.' Something was going on with her brother and the beautiful journalist, but neither of them was currently giving anything away. 'She told me the pharmaceutical company Thomas was working for have paid an exorbitant amount of money to settle out of court.'

'Are you disappointed?'

'Not at all. Especially as I have it on rather good authority that Rupert means for me to administer those funds in any way I see fit.'

He started to laugh. 'And you're going to give it all to charity?'

'Of course I am. I want that money to do some good. I suspect Thomas and his cronies will think twice before they try something like that again.'

They ate and drank in silence for a bit. 'Everyone is meeting at Rupert's for a celebratory dinner tonight,' Finn finally said.

'Excellent. It's so nice to have the whole family together.' She'd like to share her news with all of them tonight. But she had to tell Finn first. 'Do you ever regret moving to Kyanós, Finn?'

His brow furrowed. 'Not once. Never. Why?'

She shrugged. 'I just wanted to make sure you weren't pining for a faster pace of life.'

'I don't miss it at all. I have you.' His grin took on a teasing edge. '*And* I get to hang-glide.' He raised an eyebrow. 'We could sneak off to continue your training right now if you wanted.'

She'd love to, but… Her pulse started to skip. 'I'm afraid my training is going to have to go on hold for a bit.'

He leaned towards her. 'Why? You've been doing so well and…and you love it.' Uncertainty flashed across his face. 'You do love it, don't you? You're not just saying that because it's what you think I want to hear?'

'I totally love it.' She reached out to grip his hand, a smile bursting through her. 'But I'm just not confident enough in my abilities to risk it for the next nine months.'

He stared at her. She saw the exact moment the meaning of her words hit him. His jaw dropped. 'We're…we're having a baby?'

She scanned his face for any signs of uncertainty…for any consternation or dismay. Instead what she found mirrored back at her were her own excitement and love. Her joy.

He reached out to touch her face. His hands gentle and full of reverence. 'We're having a baby, Princess?'

She nodded. He drew her out of her seat to pull her into his lap. 'I—'

She could feel her own tears spill onto her cheeks at the moisture shining in his eyes. 'Amazing, isn't it?'

He nodded, his arms tightening protectively around her.

'And exciting,' she whispered, her heart full.

He nodded again. 'I don't deserve—'

She reached up and pressed her fingers to his mouth. 'You deserve every good thing, Finn Sullivan, and don't you forget it.' She pulled his head down for a kiss and it was a long time before he lifted it again. 'And they lived happily ever after,' she whispered.

He smiled, and Audra swore she could stay here in his arms forever. 'Sounds perfect.'

She had to agree that it did.

* * * * *

LET'S TALK
Romance

For exclusive extracts, competitions
and special offers, find us online:

f facebook.com/millsandboon

@ @millsandboonuk

y @millsandboon

Or get in touch on 0844 844 1351*

For all the latest titles coming soon,
visit millsandboon.co.uk/nextmonth

*Calls cost 7p per minute plus your phone company's price per
minute access charge